"I came to you for comfort and guidance," Marcus said. "I can't quite remember why."

"Stop stalling. Get to the dirt."

Marcus stopped in the middle of the path, faced Father Ballard, and crossed himself. "Forgive me, Father, for I have sinned. It has been six months since my last confession."

"What happened six months ago?"

"I met Eleanor."

The Original Sinners Series by Tiffany Reisz

Tiffany Reisz

THE CONFESSIONS

8TH CIRCLE PRESS

Trade Paperback (Limited Edition Cover) ISBN 978-1-949769-45-6

Trade Paperback ISBN 978-1-949769-30-2

Library Hardcover ISBN 978-1-949769-04-3

Cover design by Andrew Shaffer

Front and back cover images used under license from Shutterstock.com.

"The Confession of Marcus Stearns" previously published as a limited-edition paper-back in 2014.

www.8thcirclepress.com

First Edition

For Honeytoast

CONTENTS

AUTHOR'S NOTE

"The Confession of Marcus Stearns" takes place during the historical timeframe of the Original Sinners White Years novels *The Saint* and *The King*. "The Confession of Eleanor Schreiber" takes place the year before the present-day events of *The Virgin* and *The Queen*.

THE CONFESSION OF MARCUS STEARNS

"Teacher, which commandment in the law is the greatest?"

And He said to them, "You shall love the Lord, your God, with all your heart, with all your soul, and with all your mind. This is the greatest and first commandment. The second is like it: You shall love your neighbor as yourself. The whole law and the prophets depend on these two commandments."

– Matthew 22:36-40

God said, *Let there be music. And there was music.*

At least, that's what Father Ballard assumed had happened. Father Stuart Ballard took his seat in the second-to-last pew and sent a prayer skyward, a simple thank you to God for creating music. He'd come in as the choir—a university group from somewhere in Kentucky—started its second piece, a bluegrass rendition of "Be Thou My Vision."

> *Be thou my vision, O Lord of my heart*
> *Naught be all else to me, save that Thou art*
> *Thou my best thought, by day or by night*
> *Waking or sleeping, Thy presence my light*

Thy presence my light . . . Perfect words in Ballard's estimation. A perfect hymn. No wonder it was Marcus's favorite. Too bad the boy wasn't here to hear it.

Boy? *He's a man now, Stuart. Not a boy anymore,* Ballard chided himself. *Stop classifying anyone under the age of 40 as a child.* Marcus was a fully ordained priest now. He had his own parish. And yet as long as Ballard lived, he'd always picture Marcus the same way—18 years old, a shattered heart limping in his chest, baring his soul to him one dark night because, as Marcus said, "I heard something about you, Father Ballard. They say you loved someone, and she left you. I loved someone too, and he left me." And that boy had looked at him with agony in his eyes and whispered, "Can you help me?"

Father Ballard had answered the plea with a hand on top of the boy's blond head and one word.

"Yes."

Music had been the key that had unlocked the gates of the boy's labyrinthine psyche. When Marcus had entered seminary, he'd been a blond wall of intellect, of taciturn reserve. He rarely spoke unless spoken to first. He showed no inclination of even attempting to make friends. And, to make matters worse, he scared the shit out of everyone—Father Ballard included. Until that night . . . the night Ballard discovered Marcus alone in the chapel after-hours playing a haunting sonata with his eyes closed. Ballard had listened a moment, moved by the boy's talent and utter absorption. Ballard certainly knew that feeling. So he'd gone to his office, dug around for a few minutes, and returned to the chapel with his guitar, an amplifier, and sheet music. The look of cold, quiet fury Marcus had given Ballard when he'd interrupted his playing nearly sent him scurrying. But he was older by thirty years than this young whelp and stood his ground.

"Enough of that long-haired shit," Ballard said. He loved classical music but he wasn't about to let Marcus know that. "Hands like yours were created to serve the devil's music. Play."

Marcus glanced at the sheet music in front of him and looked up at Ballard with unconcealed disgust.

"Father Ballard, you must be joking," Marcus said.

"Does it look like I'm joking?"

"They print sheet music for this?"

"Just play, you pretentious snob, or else you'll be cleaning bathrooms until Christmas," Ballard ordered again as he plugged in his Gibson SG. "Consider this part of your spiritual development."

Marcus sighed so that Ballard knew he was doing this entirely against his will. But the boy had played. It took a minute or two and a few false starts before he fell into the rhythm of the song. But five minutes later the five-hundred-year-old Roman chapel was filled to the rafters with the soaring sounds of Queen's "Bohemian Rhapsody," a piece made glorious on piano and electric guitar. They didn't need words. They'd leave the singing to Freddie Mercury and the angels. After the song ended, Ballard saw something he'd never seen before and had despaired of ever seeing: Marcus smiled.

"This song is nonsensical," Marcus said as he closed the sheet music. "But the melody is rather . . ."

"Fun, Marcus. The word is 'fun.' You're 18. You're allowed to have fun."

"I didn't enter seminary to have fun," Marcus said, lowering the fallboard.

"Then you entered it for the wrong reasons. Serving God is joyful, playful, exciting. It shouldn't be a chore. It should be fun. It can be fun. Have you ever had fun in your entire life?"

"Define 'fun.' "

Ballard narrowed his eyes at him. He wanted to argue, thought about arguing. He had a few speeches he could give, a few lectures. Instead he only took a deep breath and said one word.

"Layla?" Ballard asked, hopeful. If Eric "Slowhand" Clapton couldn't get to Marcus, no one could.

Marcus paused, arched a golden eyebrow at Ballard, and raised the fallboard again. Maybe there was hope for the boy after all.

After an hour of working their way through Ballard's prodigious repertoire of rock ballads, Ballard asked Marcus who had taught him to play the piano. His mother, he answered. Slowly, as if every word hurt, Marcus told Ballard about his childhood. Marcus was a fortress of secrets, yes. But the fortress had a door and Ballard had learned the key to get inside was music. That had been the night Marcus had come to Ballard's office, broken down, and asked him to hear his confession. Ballard heard the name "Kingsley" for the first time that night. That name would become a recurring theme in Marcus's confessions.

The choir of young Kentuckians finished the hymn and gave modest smiles to the heartfelt applause. At a time such as this, Ballard felt gifted with a preview of Heaven. Here they were, a group of Kentucky college students at a church in Harlem singing a sixth century Irish hymn while an old English priest remembered the half-Danish boy who'd finally taught Ballard why he'd become a priest in the first place.

Past and present, black and white, north and south, sinner and savior, all united in worship. Now if the choir would just break into a verse or two of "Sweet Child O' Mine" Father Ballard could die happy and smile all the way to Heaven.

He sat up straighter when he sensed a presence behind him. Smiling, he glanced skyward again. "Stop paying attention to us," he whispered in his mind, a prayer God was sure to answer with a hearty "no."

Where Father Marcus Stearns was concerned, God always seemed to be paying attention.

When Ballard leaned his head back, the presence behind him leaned forward.

"Six months, Marcus," Father Ballard said, tapping his wrist as if he were noting the time. "No one goes six months without sinning."

"Do you have time for me today?"

"I might. What's her name?" he asked, his usual joke when another priest approached him for confession. Ballard looked back and saw Marcus had his rosary beads wrapped around his fingers. Something about the way he held them, tight and nervous, made Ballard's blood drop a degree or two in his veins.

"Eleanor," Marcus finally said, and the air went out of the room.

Father Ballard closed his eyes and lifted one finger to say, "Wait."

Marcus waited.

Not him, Ballard prayed. *I'm not going to lose him. Any priest but him, Lord. Any priest but him.*

After ending his prayer he rose and crooked his finger at Marcus. The blond priest rose and tucked his rosary beads into the pocket of his cassock.

Side by side they walked from the sanctuary just as the choir began "Bridge Over Troubled Waters." Good song. Guns N' Roses still would have been better.

"Do you care to walk?" Father Ballard asked and Marcus said he didn't mind. They needed to get away from the church to have this conversation. "We'll go to Trinity Cemetery. If anyone asks, we're merely paying our respects to the Astors."

"Weren't the Astors staunchly anti-Catholic?" Marcus asked.

"They're dead. Surely they've learned their lesson by now."

They didn't speak all the way to the cemetery. Ballard didn't trust himself to say anything yet, not until he'd heard the story. And talking now wouldn't have been a good idea even if he'd had the words. Too many people were aware of them to hold a private conversation. It wasn't every day that New Yorkers saw two Jesuit priests in black cassocks striding purposely up Saint Nicholas Avenue. Of course, even when Marcus wore street clothes he got looks both curious and hungry from women and men. The faces that stared at Marcus all wore the same expression, said the same thing. . . .

What a waste.

"You hate me right now, don't you?" Ballard asked him as they turned the corner and walked through the gates of the old cemetery.

"Hate is a strong word," Marcus said, a diplomatic answer from a priest not known for his diplomacy.

"The cassock sets us apart. This is a good thing. People need to identify us."

"The collar isn't enough for you?"

"Diocesan priests wear collars. Jesuits should wear cassocks."

"You and I both pastor in parish churches now," Marcus reminded him. "We aren't on the mission field."

"The world is the mission field. Also, black is slimming and the cassock makes me look taller, don't you think?" Ballard required all the Jesuits he counseled to wear a cassock in his presence. Marcus had called him a sadist for that reason. Because he knew Marcus so well, Ballard took it as a compliment.

"If you haven't noticed, looking taller is not something I need help with," Marcus said.

"Humility is, however. You hate wearing a cassock because you feel ridiculous wearing one," Ballard said.

"It's medieval," Marcus said. "You might as well walk down the street in a suit of armor."

"This is my armor," Father Ballard said and stopped at the junction of two walking paths. To his left stood an ivy-covered crypt. To his right, the tomb of Alfred Dickens, son of Charles Dickens. He and Marcus weren't the only sons of England present and accounted for in the cemetery today.

"I don't need armor," Marcus said. "I intimidate people too much as it is."

"And you like it. Also, if we were in street clothes I might be tempted to send you arse over elbow, young man. This cassock is the only thing coming between you and a bloody nose."

"The cassock and eight inches of air," Marcus said.

"I'm five-eight. That isn't short."

Marcus arched his eyebrow and looked down at him.

"Fuck the cassock," Father Ballard said. "Kneel down. I want to break your nose."

Marcus stood up straighter. "You'll be threatening to box my ears next."

"Bastard," Father Ballard said. "Remind me again why I like you so much."

"If I knew, I would tell you."

"Walk." Ballard waved his hand toward the path. "Tell me about this girl."

"You'll hear my confession?"

"I suppose I'll have to," Ballard said, following Marcus onto the path. "I certainly don't want you telling it to anyone else."

"I never considered speaking to anyone else."

"Then confess. I'll be over here praying lightning strikes us both and puts us out of our misery."

"I came to you for comfort and guidance," Marcus said. "I can't quite remember why."

"Stop stalling. Get to the dirt."

Marcus stopped in the middle of the path, faced him, and crossed himself. "Forgive me, Father, for I have sinned. It has been six months since my last confession."

"What happened six months ago?"

"I met Eleanor."

"Lovely name. I hope she's beautiful enough to warrant ruining your life over."

"She is."

Marcus said the words simply and without hesitation. Father Ballard felt a pang in his throat and a stone in his chest. He hadn't made love to a woman since becoming a priest. Forty years since he entered seminary. Thirty years since the last kiss, a kiss he bitterly regretted if only because it had been just a kiss . . . a kiss and nothing more.

"Well, that's good then. Glad to hear she's worth it." Father Ballard waved his hand and set out walking again. "Go on. Tell me all about it."

"I would prefer not to."

"Sorry, Bartleby. This is confession. No secrets here."

"I'm a priest now, ordained. I hear confession every week. I know how much a secret weighs."

"Ta, then," Ballard said, trying and failing to keep the sarcasm out of his voice. "But I'm not going to absolve you if you hide things from me."

"It's called the sacrament of reconciliation, not the sacrament of interrogation."

"If you wanted a nice easy confession, you should have gone to a Franciscan. I know some Franciscans. Lovely gents. Good confessors too, if you can get them to stop playing with their puppies and kittens long enough to bless you."

"I'm confessing to you because I trust you and I care for you. I care enough to want to spare you the details."

"Spare me your sparing of me. I can't help you until I know what's going on. You've told me a thing or two that's turned my hair gray and shaved a few years off my life. You don't get to clam up now, not when it matters most."

"I don't know where to start," Marcus said, a rare note of apprehension in his voice. But then . . . then he smiled and laughed and for one second he looked like a boy, not a man. A boy in love.

"I'll start then," Ballard said. "Ten Commandments. Have you broken any?"

"I'm still not honoring my father."

"Considering what I know about your father, that you haven't murdered him in his sleep counts as honoring him in my books. You're a priest so I'm fairly certain you're keeping the Sabbath. I'm a little afraid to ask this question, but that's why we're here. Your Eleanor?"

"Yes? My Eleanor?"

"Are you sleeping with her?" Ballard asked.

"No."

"Do you want to?"

"Yes."

"Are you sleeping with anyone?"

"No."

"Have you since your last confession?"

"No."

"Are you hurting anyone?"

"Once a week if I can make time for it. There's no intercourse."

Father Ballard exhaled. "That's a relief. I can take a full breath now. Give me a moment. I'd like to have a few of them."

"Take as many as you need."

Ballard stopped mid-step and took three deep breaths. *Thank you, Lord, for this small miracle,* he prayed with each breath.

"I was afraid of this," Father Ballard said when his heartbeat had settled into its normal rut. "You in a church in a small town. The women must fall all over themselves for you."

"It hasn't been like that," Marcus said as they resumed walking again. "No one has tried anything, flirted to excess, or attempted to seduce me. No one but Eleanor."

"She's pursuing you?"

"Like the proverbial hound of Hell."

"Passionate type. My kind of woman."

"Girl."

"Girl?"

Marcus took a breath. "She's 16."

Father Ballard stared at Marcus. "Please tell me you're joking."

"I haven't touched her. I promise."

"But you want to. And she's 16."

"I'm not an ephebophile, Stuart. If she were my age I'd be a much happier man. But she's not. That doesn't stop me from wanting her anymore than it's stopped her from pursuing me."

"You're being sexually pursued by a 16-year-old girl."

"Yes, and she's quite tenacious."

"How tenacious?"

"She snuck into my office and masturbated on my desk."

Ballard whistled, impressed.

"That's tenacious." Father Ballard considered his options. He could laugh, cry, or punch Marcus in the face. He decided to laugh. "Is this the worst of it? She's 16, she's tenacious, and you want to fuck her."

"I'm in love with her."

"That scares me more than anything," Ballard said.

"Love scares you?"

"No. You being in love scares me." Ballard led them down a shady path. "I remember those first few months after you joined the order. Marcus Aurelius himself could have learned a thing or two about stoicism from you back in those days. In public. In private, however? In my office . . ."

"I was a shipwreck," Marcus admitted. Good. Marcus had a bad habit of forgetting he was mortal. Good that he remembered his past moments of weakness. Even better that he'd admit to them.

"You told me about your father and your sister and what he did to her and what she did to you. You told me about your mother, about what happened to her and how she was taken from you. What happened to you could have destroyed you, could have destroyed any man. But none of that broke you. You fell in love with a boy at your school, and he left you—"

"And I fell apart." Marcus said the words simply, but Ballard knew it took superhuman effort to say them. The ghost of old pain lingered in his voice. He'd never met the boy Marcus had loved, but he knew so much about Kingsley from Marcus's confessions that Ballard fancied he could identify the man in a police line-up if he had to. Getting the truth out of Marcus had been like prying a stone from a child's hand only to force the fingers apart to see the diamond on his palm. Ballard remembered prying those diamonds from Marcus's hand. . . .

I never in my life dreamed I would want another boy. Then I saw him—his dark eyes, dark brown hair, and olive skin. . . .

Father Ballard . . . what if I never see him again?

Kingsley kissed me first. I punished him for it, because I was too scared to kiss him back. I thought if I started kissing him, I would never stop.

What if I never kiss him again?

Kingsley used me as a pillow. I loved waking up to find his head on my chest or my stomach or my back. He has long dark hair and he laughs when I pull it. That's how I'd wake him up, tugging on his hair. The best days were the days his laugh was the first sound I heard.

What if I never hear it again?

I was cruel to him because he liked it and because I loved it. When I told him he was beneath me, I only meant . . . I wanted him beneath me. Always.

He left me. And he never came back.

"I know you fell apart," Ballard said, the echo of Marcus's long-ago confessions still ringing in his ears. "I'm the one who put the pieces back together. I loved you then. I love you more now. I can't bear the thought of seeing you go through that again. The only thing greater than your ability to inflict suffering is your capacity to experience it. You are taking a huge risk. I'm not talking about your career now. I'm talking about your heart."

"What isn't a risk? Birth comes with a death sentence. Every breath I take could be my last. I know loving her is a risk," Marcus said, his strong jaw set and determined. "But I can't walk away from her. No one is taking care of her right now. Someone has to."

"So you are going to sleep with her?"

Marcus paused. "Not until she's older."

"Glad you're thinking this through so thoroughly," Father Ballard said. "I feel much better now. Let's wrap this up and have tea."

"You're angry."

"Of course I'm angry. You're in love with a 16-year-old girl in your parish, and I'm not supposed to be angry?"

"That isn't why you're angry."

Ballard turned and faced Marcus. "Don't do this to me. Keep your eyes out of my head. I know you. I know what you are."

"You know what I am because I told you what I am. And I can't turn it on and off with a switch. I can read you the same way I can see the tree to our left and the graves on our right. You're angry because I'm going through with it and you didn't."

"I'm not discussing her with you today," Ballard said, meaning every word.

"You are, whether you mean to or not. She's in everything you say to me. I hear her like you're speaking with her voice. You loved her. She loved you. You chose the Church. She left. And you have never forgiven yourself. You can take your regret out on me if you want, but don't pretend it's your piety talking."

Father Ballard prayed for a miracle. All he needed was eight more inches of height so he could properly finish Marcus off. They were in a cemetery already. Good place to commit murder.

"Was it really worth it?" Marcus asked and Ballard heard the compassion under the question. "Choosing your vows over the woman you loved?"

"No," Ballard said. An easy answer to a hard question. "I thought it was the right decision at the time. Thirty years later . . . no. It wasn't worth it. I could have married her, become a deacon. But I was scared. The Church was my home. It's still my home."

Marcus fell silent. Ballard had learned long ago to leave him be when silent. Whatever came after the silence was always worth the wait.

"I had a dream last night," Marcus began at last. "I dreamt I was in a desert and I saw a man and a boy standing by a large rock. The man was the boy's father. I don't know how I knew it but I knew it, the way you know things in your dreams."

Ballard nodded, not speaking, waiting for Marcus to go on.

"And the father was weeping because he had a knife in his hand and he was going to kill his son."

"You were dreaming of Abraham and Isaac."

"I was," Marcus said. "But in the dream I didn't know who they were. I didn't realize I was in a Bible story. It felt real. The sun on my face, the sand in my eyes."

"God commanded Abraham to kill his son. A hard passage for any believer."

"I watched the man raise the knife over his son's heart. I awoke with a start when he brought the knife down. I felt the knife in my own chest, Stuart."

"That must have been terrifying."

"It should have been, but it wasn't." Marcus shook his head, seemingly dumbfounded by the experience. "I felt this deep sense of joy. *It was only a test. . . .* I heard those words ringing in my head like a bell. *This has been a test.*"

Ballard smiled. "It was a test. God ordered Abraham to kill his own son Isaac—'whom you love.' I never forgot those words. The moment Abraham is fully willing to kill his son for God, when he's bringing the knife down, that's when the angel stops his hand and saves Isaac. Or rather, he saves Abraham. Saves him from having to kill his own child. But Abraham proved he was willing to make the ultimate sacrifice by killing his only son. God proved He was willing to kill His only son too. But God went through with it."

"I've never told you this," Marcus began, and Ballard had a feeling there was much Marcus had never told him. "But the night before my ordination I read that passage in Genesis. I was Abraham. Kingsley was Isaac. If I took my vows and became a priest, it would be like putting a knife through my love for Kingsley. And I had to be willing to do that. I invited him to my ordination. Did you know that?"

"Another thing you never told me."

"I sent the letter to his grandparents' address in Maine. I thought if anyone could find him, it would be them. Something told me he would be there at my ordination. He would come. I believed it so thoroughly I thought I saw him in the back of the church."

"Why did you invite him? Hoping he'd stop the wedding this time like you wish he'd done the last time?"

Marcus laughed, a mirthless laugh but a laugh nonetheless.

"I needed to prove to myself I loved God more than Kingsley. When I took my vows, I was certain he was there, watching me. I made my vows anyway. I chose God over Kingsley. I brought down the knife." Marcus stopped speaking again. Ballard saw his jaw clench. "The letter I sent came back to me the day after my ordination. Both his grandparents had died. Kingsley had left no forwarding address. He hadn't been there after all."

"But it doesn't matter. You thought he was there. You could have walked away from the Church, from the priesthood that very day and you didn't. You passed Abraham's test."

"It's a sick, sadistic thing to order a father to kill his son, isn't it?" Marcus asked. "I've played my share of mind games but I would never go so far. Even I have my limits."

"Sadistic is the word for it. God in the Old Testament wasn't anyone's pal."

"What if God's still like that? What if He's still playing games with us? What if the vows are a test? Will we give up wealth, freedom, marriage, and sex for His sake? What if we do and then along comes an angel with black hair and green eyes and green hair and black eyes and says, 'This was only a test. You passed. Put the knife down.'"

"And come to bed?"

Marcus smiled. "She would say that."

"You and I both know that's wishful thinking. I've been a priest a long time, long enough to know the vows are far more for the Church's sake than God's. It's not a popular opinion but more of us believe that than we're willing to admit. One century the sun revolves around the earth. The next century the earth revolves around the sun. We're making it up as we go along."

"So what do we do? The Church says the sun revolves around the earth so we force ourselves to believe it?"

"Of course not. We believe what we know to be true. But we do so very quietly. If you truly believe you and her belong together . . . who am I say to you're wrong? If you think you are no longer beholden to the vow you made them break it. But . . ."

"Break it quietly."

"For your sake, her sake, and the sake of the Church. Please no more scandals. My heart can't take it."

"Why do they do this to us?"

"Good reasons? They can send us anywhere without having to move whole families. We can get closer to people because there's no wife or children at home to get jealous of how much time we're spending with the sick or the scared. Bad reasons? The Church wants to control its clergy. Control the cock, control the man. We fall in love, get married, have children . . . suddenly we have something in our lives more important than the Church."

"So much for being fruitful and multiplying."

"You want to have children with her?"

"She's the freest spirit I've ever encountered. I would never burden her with a child. She is a child and always will be. Child-like, not childish."

"That's not an answer to my question. You told me about her, not about you. Do you want to have children with her?"

"I have the standard male biological urge to father a child. Considering who and what my father is, who and what I am . . ."

"You would make a wonderful father."

"I am a Father. That is enough for me."

"And that girl you love is God's child. Don't ever forget that. She was His before she was yours, and she'll be His during and after."

"I won't forget."

They walked in silence for a time, past a hundred graves or more. Someday Ballard would be in a grave and all that would be left of him on this earth would be the memory shared by those who knew him. Miriam . . . he'd leave her with too few memories. A thousand whispers. A hundred embraces. A dozen nervous phone calls. And not one single night together in his bed. He should have spent at least one night with her. It was all she'd asked. He'd made love to her a thousand times in his mind, taken her endlessly in his heart. Why hadn't he had the courage to let his body go through with it? One night and he couldn't give her that. He could have given her a good memory to cherish. Instead he'd only given them both a void in the shape of one night with the woman he loved.

"Tell me what she's like," Ballard said. "Convince me she's worth you risking your entire vocation over."

"What do you want to know? Height? Short. Hair color? Black."

"What do you see in her?"

"She . . . she makes me laugh. I feel human with her. I don't feel human very often, but I do with her."

"You are human."

"If I wasn't sure I was human before, I am now. She makes me weak."

"That's why they call this sacrament 'reconciliation.' Yes, God and sinner are reconciled. But more than that, man is reconciled with himself. We are the most ourselves when giving our confession. 'God have mercy on me a sinner.' "

"God have mercy on me a sinner," Marcus said. "And God have mercy on me because I cannot repent of loving her."

"Is she in love with you?"

"I have every reason to believe she is. Although she hasn't said the words and neither have I."

"Do you believe a 16-year-old has any idea what love is?"

"We're Catholic priests, Stuart. We believe a 14-year-old girl gave birth to the Son of God. We believe God was incarnate as that infant child. And we believe children as young as seven can partake of Communion as they've reached the age of reason."

"Nice speech. Now answer my question."

Marcus sighed heavily. "Kingsley was 16 when he fell in love with me. He's still in love with me eleven years later. If a 16-year-old can't love, how do you explain that?"

"How do you know he's still in love with you? Last time we talked you hadn't seen him in months. And even then he was unconscious in a hospital bed."

"I've seen him. I didn't want to. No—that's a lie. I didn't want to want to see him. I was avoiding it although I knew where he lived. But I had to see him."

"That must have hard for you."

"It was agony."

"Why did you do it?"

"I needed his help. We're . . . friends? Working on that."

"And now? Is it still agony?"

"Still and always."

"Because you're still in love with him." It wasn't a question.

Marcus nodded.

"So what you're telling me is that you're not only in love with this girl, but you're still in love with Kingsley who is now back in your life? Anything else?"

"Nothing else. For now."

"This is going to be a long confession."

"It was your decision to go for the walk. In August. While wearing a cassock."

"I make poor decisions sometimes," Ballard said.

"You agreed to be my confessor eleven years ago."

"And that was my first mistake."

Marcus had the decency to at least attempt to look apologetic. He didn't quite succeed but the effort was appreciated.

"I dreamed of her," Marcus said as they walked under a stone arch and into a shadier, cooler part of the cemetery. "Years ago, Kingsley and I were—"

"I don't want to hear the end of that sentence."

"Talking."

"Just talking? Good."

"I waited until we were done talking to beat him and fuck him."

"Oh God, you do this to me on purpose." Ballard winced.

"Of course I do. I'm a sadist."

"I'm the most open-minded priest I know but for God's sake, don't paint me a picture."

"You know Kingsley and I were lovers when we were teenagers. None of this is news to you."

"Knowing and picturing are two different things." Ballard raised his hand to his eyes as if to block out the mental images.

Marcus only laughed. "If Kingsley were here he'd call you a close-minded homophobic vanilla bigot. In French."

"I'm a sixty-year-old heterosexual Jesuit priest who has nothing but respect for monogamy, marriage, and the missionary position. Continue. Please."

"As I was saying . . . years ago, Kingsley and I were talking. Dreaming out loud. We were at an all-boys school, so of course we were dreaming of girls."

"Much better."

"And we imagined a girl who had black hair like his but was pale like I am. Green eyes with black hair. Green hair with black eyes. Wilder than the both of us together."

"Were you drunk?"

"Only on each other."

"I walked right into that one."

"Your own fault," Marcus said, once more unapologetic.

"Keep talking." Ballard waved his hand and tried to ignore the images in his head.

"As I was saying, we were dreaming out loud about this girl. An impossible dream. Only a dream. I thought that until I saw the dream standing in front of me waiting to take Holy Communion. . . . Have you ever recognized someone you've never met before?"

Father Ballard smiled. "I did once. Yes."

"When?"

Ballard smiled to himself. "The hour I first believed."

"It was like that," Marcus said, quieter now. "I was so shocked I almost forgot my lines."

"It's the liturgy," Ballard said, glaring at Marcus. "Not 'your lines.' This is the Catholic Church, not Shakespeare in the Park."

"It's what Eleanor calls it. She asked me recently how I remember all my lines. I thought it was . . ."

"What?"

"It was cute."

"Cute?"

"She also calls the narthex the 'lobby.' "

"Jesus, Mary and Joseph . . ." Father Ballard shook his head and crossed himself. He hadn't felt this torn since Miriam left. He loved Marcus and it was a joy to see him so happy. And yet . . .

"Marcus, I swear—"

"Stuart, you know I hate it when you call me that."

"Marcus is your name."

"Marcus is my father's name."

"It's your name too. Your issues with your father notwithstanding—"

"I have no issues with my father," Marcus said. "I hate him. That's not an issue. That is a fact."

"No issues with your father? Do you know how many white male British Catholics there are? Double digits might be wishful thinking. You can count the number of English Jesuits living in American on one hand. And yet, you, the son of an Englishman, find the one English Jesuit in the entire province to be your confessor."

"Coincidence."

"We're Catholics. We don't believe in coincidence. Does this girl of yours have a good relationship with her father?"

"No. He's a criminal. He abandoned her when she was arrested for committing a crime he forced her to commit. I've forbidden her from having any contact with him whatsoever."

"And you have no contact with your father anymore either," Ballard said. "And you've forbidden both your sisters from having any contact with him."

"I'm 29 years old, Stuart. I don't have daddy issues."

"You're six-feet-four inches of daddy issues. Your father joined the English Army. You join God's Army. Your father is a sadist. You're a sadist. Your father raped an 18-year-old girl who worked for him while he was married to someone else. You've fallen in love with a 16-year-old girl who attends your church while under a vow of celibacy."

"Are you telling me I'm becoming my father?"

"I'm telling you what you already know. God is testing you. He's testing you the same way He tested your father. Your father failed. So far you seem to be passing."

"So far."

"Go on. Tell me the whole story."

"The whole story?" Marcus sighed. "I was born, I lived, I fell in love with Kingsley. And we dreamed . . ."

Marcus spoke for a long time. He told the story of a long ago conversation between two teenage boys in love. Then a warning from his friend Magdalena in Rome who swore she could see his future. In his future she saw the girl he'd once dreamed of. Marcus told him of seeing her for the first time and recognizing her instantly and somehow she seemed to recognize him. From the very beginning they could communicate almost without words. Why? Why had God brought him into her life? Marcus had been consumed with the question for a week until the phone call from the girl's mother came. *Help,* she'd said. *Eleanor's been arrested.* Five cars stolen all at her criminal father's behest. And Marcus could help. Only he could help. But Eleanor wouldn't accept his help. Not unless Marcus made her a promise.

"Twisted your arm, did she?" Ballard asked.

"Between letting her go to juvenile detention versus telling her I'd sleep with her someday? I'll admit it was hardly Sophie's choice."

"If it had been Miriam facing jail time . . . I would have done the same thing. I can't help but wondering, however . . ."

"However?"

"However . . . your Eleanor chose being lovers with a priest fourteen years her senior who is also a sadist over a few years in detention. Out of the frying pan and into the fire, perhaps? She can't possibly know what she's getting into, choosing an affair with you. Even if she was 20, 30, being with a priest is its own sort of prison sentence."

"And that, Stuart, is why I'm here talking to you."

Marcus crossed his arms and leaned back against a crypt. The evening sunlight tangled in Marcus's blond hair. If he'd been wearing anything other than a cassock, he'd look like a male model posing for a photo shoot.

You could have been an actor, Marcus, with that face of yours, Ballard thought while looking at him. *You could have been a concert pianist. You could have been a world-renowned psychologist, a legendary academic, a groundbreaking linguist. There is no reason for you to have chosen the priesthood.* And that could only mean one thing—he hadn't chosen the priesthood.

The priesthood had chosen him. God had chosen him. And if Marcus was right and God was behind bringing him and his Eleanor together, then it could only be for one reason. It was part of His divine plan. Whatever the hell that was.

"I'll give you my confession," Ballard said, the thought stirring a memory. "When I first saw you eleven years ago, I thought the order had only let you in because you'd look good on the recruiting posters."

"The Society of Jesus has posters? I should get one for Eleanor. I'll sign it for her."

"Don't be a smartarse. You know everything is about marketing these days. Look at you—tall, handsome, a genius, a polyglot. I don't even want to know how many languages you're fluent in by now. We Jesuits are inordinately proud of our intellectual heritage and our vows of poverty. And here you are, brilliant beyond reason, handsome beyond reason, and wealthy beyond reason. You bestowed all your gifts at the foot of the cross, put on the collar, and made us look good in the process. I'm surprised they don't have you doing commercials. But then I realized something after getting to know you. When they looked at you, they saw a priest. And that's what I saw too."

Marcus smiled but didn't speak.

"I do envy you," Ballard continued, "and not for the reason you might think. When I was a boy I loved reading Doyle's Sherlock stories. I was amazed by how clever Sherlock was, deducing a man's entire life from the scuffs on his shoes. And you were like that—but for the soul. One glance at the scuff marks on the soul, and you could a man's sins. What a blessing."

"It doesn't feel a blessing most of the time."

"It's a gift—a gift tied up with a string attached. God gave it to you to use for His glory. And you do."

"I try."

"You've seen into this girl's heart, haven't you?"

"Of course I have."

"What do you see when you look at her?"

"I see. . . ." Marcus closed his eyes. "There's a spirit in her, something with wings, something that keeps her aloft, high above everything that would bring her crashing to earth. At the very heart of her is a well of joy. She has a fearlessness to her I've never encountered before. She's not afraid of me. She's not afraid of anything. She's smart, dangerous, manipulative, and utterly untamable. She is the freest person I've ever known. I couldn't get her to shut up with a ball gag and a muzzle."

"What's a ball— Wait. Don't answer that. I forget who I'm talking to sometimes."

"Apologies," Marcus said, a hand on his chest, courteous as a prince. "My point is she has no filter. I could sit back and listen to her talk for hours. If I asked her to, I think she would." He closed his eyes and released a deep breath. "I can't get enough of her."

Father Ballard stepped forward and rested his hand on Marcus's shoulder. "You're terrified, aren't you?"

Marcus slowly nodded. "I never thought I would see Kingsley again, not after that day in the hospital. When I met her, saw her the first time, I let myself love her. Completely. Unreservedly. I never meant to act on that love, only to enjoy it, rejoice in it. . . . I could be an astronomer and she every star in the night sky. We'd never touch, of course. No astronomer ever touched a star. But I could live for her light. . . . Unfortunately, my resolve to love her chastely didn't last much longer than five minutes."

"Chaste love is overrated," Ballard said, knowing that of which he spoke.

"I'm awash in love and confusion," Marcus said. "I thought I would never see Kingsley again. I let myself love her because I thought I would never see him again. And then . . ."

Ballard's pity swelled in him like a wave that crashed upon his heart. Marcus had mourned for his Kingsley with the bottomless grief of a widow. And as soon as he'd let go of his grief, let himself love anew finally . . . his lost love had come back to him.

"Marcus, my boy, you were a beautiful ruin when I met you eleven years ago. And I can't tell you the joy it gave me to see you come back to life, to see how being a Jesuit healed something inside you. I have loved you like my own child. I want you to be happy and I want you to feel joy and be loved. And I never want you to be lonely or to make the same mistakes I did. That's every good father's wish for his child—be happy, be good, don't get hurt. You are walking through a minefield, son. I can't look. But I can't look away either."

"Help me," Marcus said, the words an order and not a plea. "You've counseled dozens of priests in situations like mine. Help me do this right. For her sake."

Father Ballard stepped back and sat on top of a tombstone bearing the name of Forrest, clasped his hands between his knees, and looked upward to Heaven. God forgive him for this but he couldn't bear to let Marcus live with same regret he'd carried for thirty years.

"I was 15 my first time," Ballard said at last. "Father Mack Donnelly came to school, talked half of us into signing up, I went straight home and told my father I'd been called to be a priest. Two hours later I was sitting in the kitchen of the lovely young widow Gloria Anderson. Dad went for a walk. When he came back an hour later, I was a grinning idiot. I'd fucked that woman five times in one hour. My enthusiasm far outweighed my stamina. But what do you know? I didn't give being a priest another thought until I was 20. My father was a wise man. Then again, boys have it so much easier than girls, don't we?"

"Much," Marcus said emphatically, likely thinking of his sister.

"Can you imagine a father taking his 15-year-old daughter to get deflowered by the friendly neighborhood widower? What a job for a man that would be, eh?"

"If such a position were open, I'm certain Kingsley would volunteer."

"He'd have to stand in line." Ballard laughed and rubbed his forehead. "Poor girls. We never let them have any fun, do we?"

"That might be what I love most about Eleanor. She doesn't ask permission. She does what she wants."

"Maybe this girl can survive a life with you after all." Half a life, anyway. Although Ballard wouldn't say that out loud. He looked Marcus straight in the eyes. If he was going to do this—and Ballard knew Marcus was—he would make sure it was done right.

"Wait until she's 18," Ballard ordered. He rarely gave Marcus orders, rarely gave anyone orders. This was an order.

"I plan on waiting longer than that. The longer I wait, the more likely it is she'll let go and move on."

"Tell yourself that. Miriam's loved me thirty years." Ballard crossed his arms and looked to the ground at his own feet of clay. He looked up at Marcus and met his eyes.

"For starters, let her date other men. Encourage her to go to college. If anything will get her away from you and the Church, it's college. Whatever you do, do not get her pregnant. If you do, you leave the priesthood that day. Don't take a single night to think it over. If she gets pregnant, you call your bishop and your superior. The cover-up is always worse than the crime. Plan to get caught. You probably will get caught. When you do, you take full responsibility."

"I do take full responsibility."

"If it hits the press, she'll need a place to hide. Something like this will make the news. Make sure she has somewhere to go, or she'll end up with her pretty face on the front page of the newspapers."

"Kingsley will take care of her. He can get out of the country easily if it comes to that."

"You have friends at your church?"

"My secretary Diane. Should I warn her?"

"Does she love you? Is she loyal?"

"Yes and yes."

"Then no, don't tell her. If she's loyal, she'll lie for you. Leave her out of this. There's no way for this to happen without you committing some egregious sins. Keep them on your own head. No one else's."

"Anything else?"

"Pray for her. Pray for yourself. Pray this girl falls in love with someone else and leaves you before you do any damage."

"I've been praying that since the day I met her."

"If she wants to leave you, let her leave. I don't care if you think it'll kill you to let her go, let her. And it won't kill you. But you'll wish it did. I speak from experience."

"If she leaves, I'll let her go."

"I don't care how intelligent she is, how mature, how beautiful or insightful or whatever it is you tell yourself to justify your feelings for her—she's 16. You get caught fucking her and may God have mercy on your soul because no one else on earth will. Myself included."

"I accept that."

"Once you break the vow of celibacy with one person you'll want to break it with everyone you meet. It's like cheating on a diet. You have one bite so you tell yourself you might as well eat the whole thing. The second the vow shatters everyone will be a temptation. Don't give in. If you put this girl through the misery of being in an affair with a priest, at the very least you can give her your fidelity. Let her have whomever she wants. You stay faithful."

Marcus's gray eyes flinched. What Ballard had said hurt. Good.

"Marcus—"

"What about Kingsley?"

"What about him?"

"I love him too."

"I don't care. You get her or you get him. You'll have to choose."

"Why?"

"Because she's 16, and you're a bloody priest. She's Catholic. She's a child of God. And you're going to bring her into a sinful relationship that could ruin her life. You don't get to cheat on her as well. If you can't give her a real marriage, you can at least give her the semblance of one. No cheating."

"It's not like that in our world—"

"Fuck your world, Marcus. I live in the real world. It's fidelity or it's cheating. If she's not enough for you—"

"More than enough for me."

"Then you have your answer. You told me what you did to your beloved Kingsley. He's a child of God too and deserves better than to be hurt like you hurt him."

"I'm a sadist, and he's a masochist—"

"That's not what I was talking about. You married his sister and she died because she caught you two together. I don't care what you and he did in bed together. I care that you betrayed his love for you. He's not here to speak for himself so I will stand in his stead and speak on his behalf. You don't get to hurt him ever again. Do you understand that?"

Marcus turned his head and looked away, far away, in the distance. The sun was setting over the Manhattan skyline. The sun rises on the just and the unjust. Which were they?

"I understand," Marcus finally said.

"Good."

"Kingsley . . . I wasn't a priest when he and I were together. But she's only known me as a priest. He'll never understand why I became a priest, never accept. She will. I think she already does."

"I don't say this very often," Ballard said. "In fact, I don't think I've ever said it, but I'm saying it to you. You were born to be a priest. It's who you are and what you are and you will never be at peace if you leave the Church. It would be like cutting the wings off an angel."

"I know that. I was never at peace until I became a priest. Even now, in the midst of all this turmoil in my heart . . . I'm still at peace."

Ballard nodded. "You are at peace because you've built your house upon the Rock. The winds and waves have come now. When they pass your house will still be standing. And I'll be standing by you."

"Is loving her a sin?"

"No. Love is never a sin. If it's a sin it's not love. And if it's love it's not a sin. But that's not what you're asking. You want to know if making love to her is a sin."

"Is it?"

"I think God's view of sex is far removed from what the Church teaches. All I can say is that if the peace you know in your heart evaporates after your first night with her, you'll know you're in sin."

"If it doesn't?"

"If it doesn't then God is more forbearing than we give Him credit for," Ballard said.

"Tamar dressed like a prostitute and seduced her father-in-law. Ruth got a husband by instigating intercourse with a barely conscious Boaz on the threshing floor. King David had over a dozen wives. King Solomon had seven hundred or more—"

"And Jesus Christ had none. We aren't living in the Old Testament."

"We aren't living in the New Testament either," Marcus said. "1 Corinthians 7:9, 'But if they do not have self-control, let them marry; for it is better to marry than to burn with passion.' Seems a stark contrast to the grin and bear philosophy behind the vow of celibacy."

"No one forced you to be a priest."

"John 6:68," Marcus said as if that were the only answer. Perhaps it was.

John 6:68. Ballard knew the verse well. Many disciples had walked away from Christ and his hard teachings. To his twelve, Jesus had asked, "You do not want to go away also, do you?" And in John 6:68 Peter had answered, "Lord, to whom shall we go? You have the words of eternal life."

When it came down to it, all priests became priests for this reason—the good ones at least. Because of the love of God. Because they had nowhere else to go.

By now the sun had left them behind. At this rate they'd be walking home in the dark. But no matter. Ballard had been Marcus's confessor for eleven years now, a priest for thirty. He was a man accustomed to darkness.

"Have you ever thought . . ." Marcus began and met his eyes. "Have you ever considered, that perhaps the only thing God cares about, the only thing He wants is for us to love Him and to love each other?"

"Dangerous words, young man."

"They were Christ's words. Matthew 22: 36-40. What if He doesn't give a damn who we sleep with as long as it's consensual? I don't care what Kingsley does and with whom he does it as long as he's safe and he's happy. I have trouble believing God loves him less than I do."

"You'll put priests out of a job with thinking like that. If it was all free love and unregulated freedom, it would be anarchy."

"It would be Heaven."

"That it would be. That it would."

"I was meant to find this girl, meant to love her. God is behind this. I don't know why," Marcus said, "but this I believe."

"If you believe, then I believe. But don't fail her."

"I promise I won't."

Ballard shook his finger at him. "Don't make promises you can't keep. I know you. I watched you eviscerate an entire room of novices during a theological debate."

"It was a debate."

"We were debating *mercy*. And you showed none. You have a capacity for arrogance that borders on cruelty. And not only can you be cruel, you enjoy your own cruelty while you're inflicting it on another human being."

"That was ten years ago. I have learned a modicum of humility and self-control since then."

"Not enough. You are a dangerous man, Marcus Stearns. I'm most grateful you're a priest because I'd rather have you with us than against us. At no point should you let yourself lose control of your impulses with that girl. Not like you did with your Kingsley."

"I won't. With her or him." Marcus sounded sincere and Ballard believed that he was. But he'd seen Marcus lose his temper before, saw him reduce grown men to tears with a handful of well-chosen words. He would pray, Ballard would. He would pray for them all.

At last Ballard stood up and brushed the dirt of the dead off his shoes. He waved his hand and together they headed back toward the entrance of the cemetery.

"Will I ever get to meet this girl of yours?"

"Never," Marcus said with finality.

"No? And why not?"

"You're a flirt. Especially around well-endowed brunettes. I know you."

"I do love a curvy brunette. But give me a ginger any day. Miriam had the most beautiful long scarlet hair."

"Eleanor has long black hair. A mass of waves you could get lost in. And she smells like hothouse flowers. Black orchids and white oleander."

Father Ballard breathed in deep and tried to remember. . . . Miriam smelled like strawberries. Even her kisses tasted of them.

"Did she really get her rocks off on your desk?" Ballard asked.

"She did. And the first time we met, she called me an idiot."

"She and I would get along swimmingly. Wanking and insulting you—two of my favorite things."

"If you told me to list a hundred things I love about her right now off the top of my head . . ."

"Well?"

"I could." Marcus glanced up at the fading sun. Was he praying? Ballard hoped so. Nothing and no one but God could help him now. "I have this fantasy of waking up with her and ordering her to make the bed. She would give me a dirty look. Knowing her, she'd growl at me while she fluffed the pillows. It's not even an erotic fantasy. But the satisfaction that one mental image gives me of her glaring at me from across the bed . . . I have no words."

Marcus took a ragged breath as if that confession, his fantasy about her, had taken more out of him than any other.

"What about the erotic fantasies?" Ballard asked, a question he'd asked dozens of priests he'd counseled. Only with Marcus was he ever afraid of the answer. "Are they troubling you?"

"Yes."

"Why do they trouble you? Because she's young?"

"Because they're violent."

Marcus glanced his way for only a shamed second and turned his gaze elsewhere. Anywhere elsewhere.

"I want to tie her up, beat her black and blue, and fuck her until she bleeds. You know why that fantasy troubles me?"

"Tell me."

"Because it's the tamest one I have about her."

"I see," he said although he didn't. Marcus had explained his predilections to him a long time ago but Ballard never asked for details. He didn't need them. He certainly didn't want them. "I believe you once told me those in your community engage in a consensual sort of violence. Is that the sort of violence you're talking about? The consensual sort?"

"It's fantasy," Marcus said, his face a brick wall—hard and impenetrable. "You don't have to play by the rules in a fantasy."

"I'll take that as a 'no' then."

"It's a 'no.'"

"Well . . ." Ballard began and shrugged. "Take out the part at the ending about fucking, and you have most of my thoughts about Margaret Thatcher. Hate that woman, God forgive me. I also mentally decapitated a man who cut me off in traffic the other day. Good thing we're judged only on our actions, not our fantasies."

Marcus laughed a little. "Now I remember why I asked you to be my confessor."

"Even the most intelligent people have to be reminded of the obvious sometimes. You are not judged by what you think, but what you do. We all have horrible thoughts, thoughts that shame us, thoughts we don't even want God to see."

"It scares me, Stuart. The thoughts I have about her. I acted on a fantasy once. The first time I was with Kingsley."

"When you put him in the school infirmary for three days?"

"He could barely walk when I was done with him. He wanted it. He enjoyed it. He even thanked me for what I did to him that night and told me he loved me for the first time. Cold comfort. . . ."

"When I was 17, I got into a drunken bar fight in Liverpool. Broke a Scouser's nose. Spent a night in the nick. St. Ignatius himself—"

"I know. He was arrested for street fighting."

"Son, we're all idiots when we're teenagers. You've repented, been absolved. Don't throw God's forgiveness back in His face. Don't throw Kingsley's back in his."

"You're right. I know you are. I do accept his forgiveness, and God's. The fear of doing it again, however, to her . . ."

"Sexual repression and suppression is the reason that we have priests in parishes who belong in prisons. I tell all my priests the same thing—vow of celibacy or not, you are a sexual being. God created you to be. Honor that part of yourself. Take care of your sexuality in a healthy way. If you're having fantasies, have them. Enjoy them. Don't fight them. Don't deny them their place in your psyche. But don't give them power over you."

"Stuart, tell me the truth—if she and I become lovers at some point in the future, would it truly interfere with my ability to be a good priest?"

"Not if you don't let it. I know far too many Protestant pastors and ministers who are married with children and do God's work to believe that. There's a reason the hierarchy is notorious for looking the other way when priests have lovers, but excommunicate those who get married. Half the priests in Rome have lovers—openly. The bishops don't care who you're fucking as long as the Church comes first and they can still move you around like a chess piece. You get married and have children? Then the Church isn't first in your life anymore."

"Eleanor makes it so easy to wake up in the morning. Knowing there's the merest chance I'll see her that day compels me to church knowing at some point that day she'll be standing in my doorway telling me off about one thing or another. I am lost in my love for her."

"I want to stop you, find you, bring you back. And yet . . ." Ballard said, aching with sympathy for Marcus, for himself, for all the priests he knew who were good men who'd chosen the Church over their own hearts. "If I were your age and had it to do all over again . . ."

"Yes?"

"Well, let's just say poor Miriam would wear out her knees from a certain activity that is not related to praying."

"I didn't need that image in my head."

"Turnabout is fair play, my boy."

They talked of other things all the way back to the church. Music mostly. Marcus had been invited to join a chamber orchestra. Ballard had been given tickets to an Aerosmith concert by a friend. Marcus asked him if he knew anything about a band called Pearl Jam. Better guitar-playing than Nirvana, Ballard informed him, but that wasn't saying much. When they arrived back at church they stood in the narthex by the altar. Ballard lit a candle and raised it in a salute.

"For her. I'll be praying for her," Ballard said.

"I thank you on her behalf. I have yet to stop praying for her." Marcus lifted a match and lit a candle of his own.

"Who is that for?" Ballard asked.

"Your Miriam," he said.

Ballard swallowed a sudden lump in his throat. Miriam O'Donnell—red hair, blue eyes, a dirty laugh, a wide smile, and a heart that was born to love him. As much as he'd loved her, when he had to choose, he'd picked the Church over her. As much as he'd pined for her, questioned his choice, wished things had been different, when the time came to look God in the face, Ballard would say if he had to do it over again, he still would have become a priest.

"I dream sometimes about going back in time, marrying her, having children. When I imagine having a son, he's very much like you," Ballard said. "Only shorter. Less arrogant. Not blond."

"So nothing like me then?"

"Not a bit. Now get out of here before I do something foolish like hug you and tell you I'll always love you no matter what happens."

"You have to absolve me first. Don't forget that part."

"I can't absolve you until you actually tell me a sin you've committed. Wanting to commit a sin isn't the same as committing one. Tell me something you're sorry for even if you have to make it up."

"I'm sorry for hurting you," Marcus said, and his eyes showed his sincerity. "I'm sorry for scaring you. I'm sorry for any scandal I might cause the Church. But I'm not sorry for finding her and loving her. I will never repent of accepting the gifts God gives me. Even if they do come with strings attached."

Marcus stood up straight again and took a step forward. Ballard looked up and into his eyes.

"I absolve you in the name of the Father, the Son, and the Holy Spirit," he said, blessing the young priest who stood before him.

"Thank you," Marcus said.

"Don't thank me. I'm only doing my job."

"Penance?" Marcus asked.

"No penance." Ballard gave him a sad and knowing smile. "Something tells me that loving your Eleanor will be penance enough."

THE CONFESSION OF
ELEANOR SCHREIBER

The Lord is the keeper of little ones: I was little and he delivered me.

– Psalm 114:6

November 2014, New York City, St. Francis Xavier Parish

Father Stuart Ballard, S.J. was 81 years old, but even if he were 91, 101, dead, he'd still notice the gams on that gal. He paused in the hallway by the door to the men's room and stared at the legs in question for a few extra seconds. Anyone who walked past him would assume poor Father Ballard needed to take a little breather. *Getting on in years, wasn't he?* Well, let them think he was too tired to walk down a long hallway without taking a break. They didn't need to know he had his eye on the nicest pair of legs he'd seen since the Clinton administration. Funny that no one ever told him when he was a kid that at 81 he'd still feel like a kid. In his mind he might as well have been 21 for the thoughts he had sometimes, especially when confronted with two shapely legs in black stockings and black high heels. He was sure there was a fancy name for the shoes she wore—slingbacks or stilettos or something like that— but it didn't matter to him what brand they were or what style. He just knew he liked what he saw. Especially since it was late-November and every good pair of legs in the city was hidden under long skirts and boots. A woman who wore high heels in the snow—he liked her already.

Lord, I am not worthy that you should enter under my roof, he prayed the old prayer in his mind. *But only say the word and my soul shall be healed. And while you're at it,* he added, *say the word and get my mind out of the gutter too, if you would, please.*

Father Ballard reminded himself that even ladies with nice legs were beloved children of God deserving of all respect due God's only Son. With that thought in mind, he straightened up and walked toward the door at the end of the hall. He tried not to look at the woman sitting outside the confessional—at her short skirt, at those legs that could make a man forget a few of the vows he'd taken over the years. Images became thoughts and thoughts became desires and desires became actions. . . . Ah, who was he kidding? He was 81. He could look at a pretty girl if he wanted to and if anyone caught him staring he'd blame it on his old eyes (without mentioning his old eyes could still see 20/20).

"You here for me, Miss?" he asked, after unlocking the door.

She looked up from the book she'd been reading, took off her glasses, and smiled at him. No girl this one. Oh no, this was a woman, a grown woman, and a beautiful grown woman at that. Black hair pinned up in a style he hadn't seen on a woman since he was a boy, dark eyes, and a full bottom lip that surely had survived its fair share of kisses. He guessed she was in her mid-thirties but these days any woman between 30 and 50 looked about the same age to him.

"I think you're here for me," she said, gathering her handbag and coat.

"Am I?" he asked.

"Saturday, four o'clock, the sacrament of reconciliation, yes?"

"Yes, Ma'am. Pull up your sins and make yourself at home."

She followed him into the small room that served as the church's confessional. The old two-parter booths weren't in use much anymore. It wasn't "confession" so much anymore but "reconciliation." Priest and penitent sat in chairs facing each other and Stuart had gone to great lengths to make sure his confessional was as comfortable and inviting as possible. Priests liked repeat customers after all.

"Leather chairs," the lady said, nodding her approval. She ran her hand over the back of the chair, scarlet red fingernails stark against the chocolate brown. "Very nice."

"Have a seat, please," he said as he took his chair by the floor lamp. "Oh, could you put the sign on the door first? You can lock the door if you like, but you don't have to. No one will interrupt." As she walked to the door, he lit a handful of votive candles on the low altar of the prie-dieu and switched on his iPod.

"Mood music?" she asked. "Never had mood music played during confession before. What do you have there? Gregorian chant? Bach?"

"Enya," Father Ballard said.

The woman burst out laughing. It was such a wide open laugh that it made him sit up straighter.

She pointed at him and shook her finger. "You surprise me," she said. "Takes a lot to do that. Now I have to revise a few mental pictures I had. . . ."

"I like to make my penitents comfortable. Plus, it's pretty, relaxing, and masks our voices. Speaker's by the door. If anyone wanted to listen to us, all they'd hear is music."

"I like it," she said. "I play music during sessions with my clients. It does help them relax. Never Enya though. I'll try that next time."

She took the sign off the back of the doorknob, read it, and raised her eyebrow.

"'Do not disturb,'" she read the sign. "'Courtesy, The Sauveterre.' That's a five-star hotel, Father. What's a Jesuit priest doing with a hotel sign from a five-star hotel?"

"Stole it," he said. "Don't worry. I've confessed that sin and been absolved."

"Met your girlfriend there?" she asked as she hung the sign on the outer doorknob before shutting the door and locking it.

"I wish," he said, watching as she took her seat across from him. He tried not to watch as she crossed her legs.

But he did anyway.

"Yes," she said with something like sympathy in her voice. "I bet you do."

"Conference," he said quickly. "The Ecumenical Council of America met at the Sauveterre three years ago. They asked me to speak there. Free night at a five-star hotel? Couldn't turn that down, could I? Stole the sign, but I left the towels."

"Sauveterre—it means 'safe haven' in French."

"That's where you are right now, dear. A safe haven. You seem to know the Sauve well."

"Very well," she said, sitting back in the chair. "I've met clients there before."

"Second time you've mentioned clients," he said. "You're a therapist?"

"We'll get to that. Should we begin?"

He looked at her a moment before leaning forward and meeting her gaze again. She looked back at him with wide eyes, a slight smile on her lips, and not a blush to be found on her pale cheeks or a tear in her eyes. If he had to describe this woman's expression, he might pick "confident" or "fearless" . . . but if he could choose only one word, he'd probably pick "shameless." Interesting expression on the face of a woman who was ostensibly here to confess her sins.

"We should begin, yes," he said. "Let's pray."

Obediently she crossed herself, closed her eyes and bowed her head.

"Glory be to the Father, and the Son and the Holy Spirit, as it was in the beginning is now and ever shall be world without end. Amen," he said.

"Amen," she said, crossing herself and raising her head. "I like it better in Latin though."

"Say it," he said.

"*Gloria patri,*" she began without a moment's hesitation, "*et Filio, et Spiritui Sancto. Sicut erat in principio, et nunc, et semper, et in saecula saeculorum. Amen.*"

"Very good." Father Ballard clapped. "Accent could use some work."

"Considering Latin's a dead language, isn't my guess at an accent as good as anyone's?"

"Not a bad point. You're too young to have grown up with the old Latin Rite. Where'd you learn it?"

"My priest," she said. "He can be a little old school."

"Nothing wrong with the old school," he said. "I can be a little old school myself."

"You're playing Enya on an iPod Nano in a confessional that looks like a Park Avenue psychotherapist's office. Leather chairs, candles, and if I'm not mistaken . . . that's a bowl of Jolly Ranchers on the table next to you."

"So I'm a little old school and a little new school. I know Latin, I wear a cassock, but I can still appreciate the power of a little candy to get a nervous child talking."

"Or a nervous woman?"

"Or that," he said, passing her the bowl of candy. She took one—cherry—but didn't eat it. "Although something tells me you aren't nervous. Am I wrong?"

He set the bowl back down on the table and faced her. Funny, he thought she had dark eyes, dark brown eyes, but now her eyes looked green. Not hazel, no. Real green. Contact lenses? A trick of the light?

"No, not nervous. I'd rather not be here, but here I am."

"If you don't want to be here, why are you here?"

"To keep a promise I made to someone," she said. "I've been putting off coming here."

"Tell me about this promise."

"My mother died two years ago. On her death bed, she asked me to go to confession and be absolved and reconciled. She was very specific about what sins I needed to confess. So here I am doing as my mother asked. Mom, I hope you're happy." She glanced up at the ceiling and shook her head in amusement. Looking up was a good sign. Meant that this lady thought her mother had gone to Heaven.

"I'm very sorry about the loss of your mother. What's her name? I'll pray for her."

"Sister Mary John," the woman said.

"A nun?"

She nodded. "She joined the Monican Order when I was in my twenties. It had been her lifelong dream. She was happy there. First time in her life she was truly happy."

"She wasn't happy before then?"

"No, but a lot of that is my fault. I was a disappointment to her."

"I find that hard to believe."

"Believe it," she said. "I'm being unfair really. She got pregnant with me as a teenager and that ended her convent dreams. I suppose she was a disappointment to herself, and I was the living manifestation of that disappointment. But we were . . . better? I suppose you could say we were better by the end. I knew she loved me. That's why I made her the promise. My sins weighed very heavily on her."

"Is this your first confession?"

"Not by a long shot. I have a priest I confess to once every few months."

"But that wasn't good enough for your mother?"

"She didn't like my priest. Thought he was a sinner."

"Doesn't matter. *Ex opera operato.* The sacrament works because of Christ and *through* the minister, not *because* of the minister. As long as your priest is a priest, he can administer the sacraments, no matter the sins on his conscience."

"Mom knew all that. But this case was a little different."

"How so?"

"Because I'm sleeping with my priest."

Clients.

Hotel.

Black eyes that turn green.

Black hair.

Shameless.

"Well, well, well," Stuart said, leaning back in his chair. "We meet at last, don't we? I have to say . . . I thought you'd be taller."

"I get that a lot. I have a tall personality."

"You are as beautiful as he said you were. I give him credit. To think I accused him of exaggerating. Then again, he's not so bad himself, is he?"

"If you're into six-foot-four blond men with perfect faces and asses you can bounce quarters off of."

"I hope you're being literal." He laughed at the image of this lovely lady flicking coins at Marcus's backside.

"It was a half-dollar actually. I like a challenge."

"So. . . ." he sat back in his chair again, crossed his ankle over his knee. Usually arthritis prevented him from sitting so casually but he was feeling good today and even better now. "Do I call you Eleanor? Or do you prefer Nora?"

She grinned broadly, brightly, and laughed.

"What does he call me?"

"Eleanor."

"Does he talk about me much?"

He ran his fingers over his lips as if zipping a zipper, then turned the imaginary key in the imaginary lock and threw the key back over his shoulder.

"I know, I know," she said. "You aren't allowed to tell me anything Søren said during his confessions. Trust me, I know the rules by now. He and I have been sleeping together, oh . . . almost years?"

"Søren. I could never get used to calling him that. He'll always be Marcus to me."

"Whereas I can't imagine calling him Marcus. It's not his name to me at all. Never has been. He told me his name the day we met."

"The day you met? Took him years before he told me what his mother named him. By then it was too late—it was Marcus."

"No, he's definitely Søren. Good Danish name. Means 'stern.' Fitting name."

"Marcus, from the Roman god of war, Mars. Even more fitting."

"For a pacifist priest?"

"He's been at war with his own soul since the night he was born, and you know it."

She glanced at the orchid on the windowsill, and then raised her hand to touch its fragile petals.

"I know it," she said softly and lowered her hand.

"And perhaps," Father Ballard continued, "you have been a casualty in this war?"

"A few cuts and bruises. Nothing fatal."

"Pressed but not crushed," he said.

"Exactly."

"Although . . ." He paused and narrowed his eyes at her. "Maybe a little crushed?"

"Maybe a little."

She took a breath and turned to face him again. She crossed her legs and sat back in the chair. They stared at each other.

"Tell me your sins, Eleanor. Let me help you find peace."

"I told you—I'm sleeping with a Jesuit priest."

"You're here to be absolved of your sin of fornication with a member of the clergy? That's it?"

"I am. Is that not a good enough sin?"

"No, it's a fine sin. One of the better sins there is. Still packs a punch. Nobody cares about adultery anymore. That's old news. But getting your rocks off with one of us? That's nice and punchy. But here's the problem: Something tells me you intend to keep sleeping with him. Yes?"

"Well . . . yes."

"Then I don't think I can help you. Usually when you confess a sin, the sinner at least tries to pretend he or she doesn't want to do it again."

"I wouldn't want to lie in confession. My mother asked me to confess my sins to a priest who is not Søren. She wanted me to be absolved of my sin of seducing a priest and/or being seduced by a priest—it changed depending on which one of us she was angrier at that day. Sometimes I was the harlot, and he was the innocent victim of my seductions. Other days he was a sexual predator and I her virginal daughter, who'd had her innocence cruelly plucked from her by a wicked clergyman. Either way it sounds so lurid and gothic, doesn't it? She never did believe the truth."

"What is the truth?"

"We were nothing but two people who fell in love with each other and did what people in love do, namely have sex with each other. Often. It was inconvenient I was so young when we met. It was even more inconvenient he was a priest. But I'm not young anymore. I still love him, and he still loves me. And we still have sex. Among other things."

Stuart waved his hand dismissively.

"You don't have to tell me what the 'other things' are. I've been hearing his confessions since he was 18. I'm actually only 60 years old. I only look 80 because of him," Ballard said.

"Liar," she said.

"I am."

"I'm only doing what my mother asked. I came to a priest who is not Søren, Marcus, whoever he is, and I'm giving you my confession. Can you absolve me so I can put that promise to rest?"

"Surely there is something you can repent of that you don't plan on doing again the minute you leave this room?"

"Not the very minute I leave the room. My flight home isn't until tomorrow. I'm only in New York for the weekend to see a special client."

"How about that? Do you repent of your work with your clients?"

"No, sorry," she said with a sigh. "I love being a Dominatrix. And I don't have sex with my clients. I'm basically a massage therapist—except instead of using my hands, I use canes and whips and floggers. It's deep tissue massage. Very deep tissue."

"Well . . . have you killed anyone?"

"Not since my last confession."

"That's a comfort, I suppose. Committed adultery?"

"No. I mean, I have, but not recently. I've confessed, been absolved. Old news, like you said."

"You're a busy lady."

"The busiest."

"Keeping the Sabbath?"

"I do go to Mass and take Communion at least once a week."

"You're honoring your mother right now by coming to me to confess as she asked you to. What about honoring your father?"

"He's also dead."

"Well, screw that Commandment then. Hmm . . ."

"You're fun," she said. "I like you."

"No flirting, wicked girl. I know I'm your type."

"I can't help it," she said. "I spread for Roman collars. What are the other Commandments again? I'm sure I've broken one of them."

"Have you coveted your neighbor's ass?"

"My neighbor is a very nice older lady who always calls me Nellie for some reason and as much as I like Mrs. Mendez, I do not covet her ass."

"Have you born false witness against anyone?"

"I've never been sure exactly what that means."

"Complicated, I suppose. Most white lying is a venial sin. I think it's only a mortal sin if you lie under oath against someone."

"Haven't done that either. Lies of omission? Søren doesn't know I'm here."

"Venial." He wished he had his Catechism with him. If he remembered correctly, he'd left it in the bathroom on the back of the toilet. "Have you made any graven images and worshiped them?"

"I'm too lazy to be an idolater. No golden calves in my house. I do have a porcelain cat with ruby eyes—real rubies, a gift from a client—but I don't worship it. It's a miracle if I remember to dust it."

"Do you take the Lord's name in vain?"

"I'm Catholic. Of course I do, God dammit."

"You'll have to do better than that for a mortal sin. Have you stolen anything?"

"Only hearts."

"You're a tough nut to crack, young lady."

"Aww . . . you called me 'young lady.' That made my day."

"I'm supposed to be shriving you, not stroking your ego. You have to give me a sin, a real one. Did we cover them all?" He raised his hands and started ticking numbers off on his fingers. "No other gods—check. No graven images—check. I don't count having a dirty mouth as taking the Lord's name in vain."

"Thank God."

"You remember the Sabbath Day—check. You can't honor your mother and father because they're dead. Haven't killed anyone since your last confession. Or committed adultery. Or stolen. Or bore false witness. Or coveted your neighbor's ass. No coveting your neighbor's wife?"

"Who counts as my neighbor again?"

"Everyone on earth, my dear."

"We might have a problem then."

"About bloody time. Tell me about your neighbor's wife. Do you fancy her? I hope so. Spare no detail."

She laughed softly and shook her head. "It's not like that. Although she is . . . she's very beautiful."

"And you covet her?"

"Not carnally."

"I'm gutted. How is it then?"

"It's complicated. I don't even know what I'm confessing. I just . . . I want to talk about it with someone, and I can't talk about it with him. Or with her. Or with the other him. Or the other him."

"How many hims do you have?"

"Søren, Kingsley, Zach, and Nico. I can't tell Søren because it's about him. I can't tell Kingsley because Søren wouldn't want me to tell him about this particular situation. I can't tell Zach because it's about his wife, and I can't tell Nico because I keep my relationship with him separate from my relationship with Søren and vice versa. I need a new him to talk to. So . . . you're him."

"You have as many hims as a hymnal."

"You're telling me, Father."

"Let's start at the beginning. This lady in question—what's her name?"

"Her name is Grace."

"Ah . . . now we're getting somewhere."

"He's told you about her? About his son?"

"You know I can't answer that," Stuart said, nodding his head in the affirmative.

"You're very good at keeping secrets. So you know who Grace is. And you know she had his son."

"You just told me so if I didn't know before, I'd know now. Let's leave it at that. Envy is a sin. Do you envy her for having his child?"

"No," she said, waving her hand. "It's not like that at all. Although I asked myself that a few times just to make sure."

"Why don't you envy her? Most women would, I think. I assume. I could be wrong. Never been a woman, much to my everlasting regret."

"Sorry about that. I've certainly enjoyed being a woman. I recommend the experience."

"I believe—and correct me if I'm wrong—that women often desire to have the children of their lovers?"

"They do, yes, sometimes. And their lovers often desire to father their lovers' children. But I don't want children. I haven't felt any strong desire to have children since I was a teenager and maybe not even then, although I certainly fantasied about it. I fantasied about a lot of things as a teenager. But now I can't even have kids."

"Can't or won't?"

"Can't. I had a sterilization procedure done recently while I was in France. It's hard to talk American doctors into sterilizing a woman without children. The French are more open-minded."

Marcus hadn't told him about this. He wondered if Marcus knew. "Surgical procedure? Was that a difficult decision?"

"It was a terrifying decision, but not for the reason you might think. I had a pregnancy scare which quickly turned into a cancer scare. Turns out it was nothing but a large fibroid tumor that needed removing." Her eyes flashed with remembered fear. "When I was nearly as relieved that I wasn't pregnant as I was that it wasn't cancer, I knew I should probably take care of both at once. So I did."

"Did Marcus know?"

"About the pregnancy scare and the cancer scare? No," she said. "Not until it was all over."

"Who did you lean on during that time?"

"Nico, my lover in France. He handles this sort of stuff better than Søren does. Nico is the eye of any storm. Søren's the storm. I didn't need a storm then. I needed the calm."

"Was Marcus angry you hadn't told him?"

"I'm sure he wasn't thrilled, but the relief was greater than the anger. He and Nico have an understanding. Søren knows when I'm with Nico, I'm with Nico, 100 percent. Nico knows when I'm with Søren, I'm with Søren, 100 percent. I don't call Søren from Nico's house. I don't write Nico love letters when Søren's asleep in bed next to me. We call it the Separation of Church and State. It's working well so far for all of us. A pregnancy would be disastrous, though, especially not knowing which one of them was the father. I'd never been more scared. That's why I went ahead and had the procedure. I know the Church sees it as a sin. I'll tell you what I told a nun once who called me out for my pride: *Put it on my tab*."

"Yes, yes, the Church frowns on birth control," he said without much conviction. Children starving in this world and the bigwig bishops still wrung their old liver-spotted hands about contraception and family planning—nonsense. Absolute nonsense. When it came to sins, he had bigger fish to fry.

"So you don't want children," he said with a shrug. "That's fine. I don't have any children myself. Not for me. Not for you. What is it then? You said you covet your neighbor's wife. Is it because Marcus and Grace made love?"

There it was, that laugh again. Big laugh. Beautiful laugh. He hadn't known he'd made a joke but apparently he had.

"That's another no," she said once she stopped laughing. "I do not feel any jealously because they slept together one time on one night. If you knew how many men—and women—I'd been with in my life . . ."

"Ballpark? You're not the only nosy one in the room."

"More than fifty. Less than a hundred," she said. "Not counting clients."

"Quite a ballpark you have there."

"Whereas he's slept with four people in his entire life. Four."

"Those four meant something to him. Did your ballpark?"

"Of course. I don't have casual sex."

"You know what I mean. You weren't in love with everyone you've been with?"

"No. And neither was he in love with his four. So it isn't jealousy. We don't do jealously like vanilla people. When I think about Søren with Kingsley, it's arousing. Two beautiful men together? There isn't anything not sexy about that. They love each other and I love them both. Same with Grace. Grace is a beautiful woman, inside and out, and one of my dearest friends. The wife of a man I love more than I'm comfortable admitting to anyone but you." Her eyes flashed again, changed color, and it seemed she was remembering something both dark and beautiful. He wished he could see into her mind. What a show that would be. . . .

"And Grace," Eleanor continued. "She loves Søren the way he deserves to be loved—unreservedly and with full faith in him. I couldn't have picked a better woman to be the mother of his child. But even knowing that, believing that, and loving her and loving him and—on top of all that—loving Fionn more than I thought was possible to love a child who isn't your own . . . there's still this thing, here." She tapped her chest over her hidden heart. "And I don't know what it is other than it hurts. So I know there's a sin in there somewhere."

"A lot of things hurt that aren't sins. Longing isn't a sin. Regret isn't a sin. Hope isn't a sin. They all hurt."

"It's not any of those. So what is it?" She rubbed her temples and looked tired—tired but lovely. It hurt his heart to see it.

"Tell me when you feel it the most, dear. Tell me when you first felt that . . ." He tapped his own chest. "That ache right there."

She sighed and leaned forward in her chair, crossing her legs at the ankles. She looked so elegant, so much like a lady. Was this really Marcus's Eleanor? The teenaged car thief who'd made off with his heart twenty-three years ago? She looked more like a duchess than a car thief.

"Ah, fuck it," she said, leaning back in the chair again. She threw one leg over the chair arm and threw her arm over her eyes to hide from him.

All right. So it was that Eleanor.

"Eleanor. Talk to me."

"He's going to kill me for telling you this."

"He won't ever know you told me."

"You promise?"

"I swear. I'm an old man with no reason to lie. I'll guard your secret with my life."

She groaned or maybe it wasn't a groan. Maybe it was a growl. *You must drive him mad*, Stuart thought. *You must make him wild for you. You are a teenage girl in a woman's body with a woman's needs and a teenage girl's savage heart.*

If he were forty years younger . . .

"I found a picture," she said at last. "I didn't mean to find it. I wasn't looking for it. I just found it. Last week."

"This all started last week?"

"Yes."

"Because you found a photograph?"

Behind the arm draped over her eyes she nodded.

"Where did you find it?" Ballard asked.

"In his old Bible. He keeps private things in it—love notes from Kingsley from their high school days, the bookmark I made him once, the list of questions I wrote for him when I was 16 that he promised to answer for me one day . . . All his most special secrets he keeps in this Bible. He left it at my house one night, and I flipped through it for no other reason than plain heathen nosiness. Is nosiness a sin?"

"Venial."

"Shit."

"Keep talking. You found the photograph in his Bible?"

"I did. Of her."

"Of Grace."

"Yes. Of Grace holding Fionn. As a baby. He's a toddler now, but he was a baby in the picture. And on the back of the photograph Grace had written the date and a short message."

"What did it say?"

"Grace wrote, *Søren, Here's the picture you asked for. It's in black and white because I'm blushing so much. All our love, Your Grace and Fionn.*"

"Is that what bothered you? That she called herself *his* Grace?"

"No, she does that even with me: *Nora, Miss you! Come visit us soon. Love, Your Grace.* It's a joke."

"Ah—'Your Grace.' Aristocracy nonsense. So what's wrong then? That he asked for the picture? It's really not unusual for the father of a child to want to have a picture of his child. He hasn't met his boy yet, has he?"

"Not yet. Next year. Søren wants to wait for reasons he hasn't told anyone. I think he wants Fionn to be old enough to remember him in case, you know."

"In case it's their only meeting?"

She nodded, swallowed visibly. He had touched a nerve, a soft spot. Good. It meant they were getting closer to the heart of the matter.

"A photograph of his son in his Bible shouldn't be much of a surprise. So why did it bother you so much?"

"The picture is of Grace nursing Fionn."

"Ah, I see." Stuart nodded and rubbed his chin in understanding. "A very private and intimate picture. Hence the blushing."

"A private and intimate picture he asked her to send him. And that's a big deal because Grace is so modest that she never nursed Fionn in public. She never even nursed him in front of me or her own mother. Only alone or in front of Zach, her husband."

"And in that photograph."

"A photograph which he kept in his Bible along with Kingsley's love notes and my list of questions and the bookmark I made him. He keeps his heart in that Bible. There are no other pictures in there, and we have dozens of pictures of Fionn. But that picture . . ."

"That must have stung," Stuart said, employing the art of the English understatement.

"Stung? Ever had your genitals whacked with a wet whip?" she asked.

"That bad?"

"That bad. And the worst part?" Eleanor sat up again and faced him. "I don't even know why it bothers me. It's a beautiful picture. Absolutely gorgeous. Grace is luminous in it. Fionn is . . . a miracle. And even more than that, he's Søren's son. Of course he wants to keep a picture of Grace and his son in his Bible. I just didn't expect it to be *that* picture. I just . . ." She held up her hands. "I didn't expect to find it in his Bible. If he'd shown it to me, it wouldn't have hurt. But he didn't show it to me. Why can't he hide creepy fetish porn from me like a normal boyfriend?"

"Did you just use the words 'normal' and 'boyfriend' when referring to Marcus?"

"I forgot myself. Sorry."

"Let me ask you this—do you think he was deliberately concealing this photograph from you? Or had he simply not shown it to you yet?"

"If he were deliberating hiding it from me, he wouldn't have put it in his Bible. If he wanted to hide it from me he would have kept it in his room at the Jesuit house. No women allowed in there."

"So he wasn't hiding it from you but he never showed it to you?"

"Which doesn't necessarily mean anything other than he wanted to protect Grace's privacy. Except it does mean something because it's in his Bible. And it's the mother of his child with his child and she's nursing him. I just wish I knew why it hurt. I don't want kids. I was overjoyed when I learned about Fionn. I wasn't shocked at all they'd slept together, considering what we'd all just been through. I even sent her to him. And, to be perfectly frank—"

"Please, be frank."

"While they were together, I was in the next room fucking Kingsley, and Wes was fucking Søren's niece Laila down the hall. Your typical post-traumatic event life-affirming fuck fest, right?"

"But of course."

"I'm not jealous they slept together—God knows they both needed each other that night. I'm not jealous she had Fionn. I'm not jealous they had a child together, and that I didn't have his child. So what is it? It's not like me to not know myself. Why do I feel this way? Why does this hurt? I'm losing it, Father Ballard. No, I've lost it."

He might have laughed at her words if he hadn't seen the look in her eyes. This was a woman in pain. "You know, a wise man once said, 'Pain is knowledge rushing in to fill a gap.' "

"Pain is knowledge rushing in to fill a gap," she repeated. "Sounds like St. Ignatius."

"Jerry Seinfeld actually."

Her eyes widened and she looked at him with new appreciative eyes. "You're his opposite, you know. You and Søren? You are ontological opposites."

"I know him well enough to take that as a compliment."

She put her hand on her forehead and exhaled heavily. "It's a compliment," she said. "It's definitely a compliment."

Stuart stood and she looked up at him in a question.

"Sit, sit," he said. "Stay there."

He picked up his chair and moved it closer to her. When he sat again she had composed her face back into that beautiful mask but the pain was still in her eyes. He reached out and held open his hands to her. She slipped her hands into his and he held her trembling fingers.

"Pain is knowledge," Stuart said again. "Adam and Eve fell when they ate from the Tree of Knowledge. That fall hurt. You saw that picture and it was a bite of knowledge that you wish you'd never tasted. Isn't it?"

"It could be."

"You were walking along and ran into something you didn't know was there. And it hurt the way it always hurts when you walk into something you didn't see in your path—a doorknob, a chair leg, a secret your lover of nearly twenty years was keeping from you. You didn't stub your toe here, however. You stubbed your soul."

"He never told me he wanted that—that in the picture. He never said a word about it," she said.

"If he had, what would have happened? If five years ago, let's say, he sat you down in his living room and said, 'Eleanor, I want you to have my children.' What would you have said to that?"

She shrugged. "I don't know. I do know I wouldn't have had his children. Not even for him would I have had a child I didn't want to have."

"If he had asked you, would you have said no right away? Or would you have had to think about it?"

"I wouldn't have said no right away. As much as I love him, I would have at least thought about it, if I could go through with it, if I could change who I was enough to be something I didn't want to be."

"And when you told him no, would that have been an easy conversation?"

She whispered her one-word answer. "No."

"Why not? Yes or no is such an easy answer."

"Not when the question is 'Will you have my children?' The no would have been as hard to say as the yes."

"Do you think he wanted to spare you that? Do you think he was trying to protect you from having to answer that question?"

"I'm sure he was."

"And that photograph you found . . . that photograph he keeps among his most private and cherished possessions . . . when you saw it, perhaps you saw a side of him you didn't know was there. The side of him that does want, you know . . ." Stuart's voice trailed off. It was better to let her say it.

"He wants to see the mother of his child nursing his son."

"That," he said.

"It's something I could never give him. Maybe that's why it hurts. I don't know." She closed her eyes again.

"It hurts when we realize we can't give everything to the person we love, that we can't be everything to the person we love."

"It hurts," she said, nodding.

"You had a gap in your knowledge of him. And that must have hurt because surely after so many years together you would know his soul by heart. But you don't know everything there is to know about him. You learned he had a side of himself he never shared with you."

"I thought I knew everything. I thought we'd reached that point where we were honest with each other, truly honest. After all we've been through—"

"After all you two have been through, it's a miracle you can even be in the same room together, much less still in love with each other. Devotedly and passionately in love."

She gave him a wan smile. Such a pretty girl. No wonder Marcus couldn't get enough of her even after decades of loving her.

"I have to remember I'm his lover, not his confessor," she said.

"I am his confessor, lass. Even I don't know all his secrets. And I don't want to know them. You see all this gray hair? Each strand is one of his bloody secrets."

She smiled again, but didn't laugh. He could tell she wasn't quite ready to laugh yet. But they were getting there.

"How do you think you sinned here?" he asked her. "Do you think it's a sin for a woman to not want children?"

"I spent a year in a convent with women who didn't want children, and they were some of the godliest women I've ever known."

"Do you think it's a sin that a tiny part of you wishes you could have been everything to him?"

"Yes, I think that is a sin," she said. "Pride. Thinking I'm enough to be everything to him. And I'm not. I already knew that because of Kingsley, but I've known about Kingsley for decades. Kingsley was Søren's first love, and I respect his primacy. But this is different."

"It is different. Kingsley is a man," Stuart continued. "He can't have children. You're a woman. You can. And you chose not to, and now he's had a child with someone else. You love the woman. You love the child. You love him. But . . ."

"But." She squeezed his hands in hers. The girl had a strong grip. Lots of hidden strengths in this lady. No wonder she'd survived so long with Marcus. "Once upon a time I said something breathtakingly cruel to Søren."

"What did you say?"

"We were standing in his church and we . . . we'd been broken up for a few years by then. There were children everywhere, all around us. They were doing something—practicing for the Easter pageant, I think. Anyway, here we were, broken up and he wanted me back, a very vulnerable, horrible, hard place for anyone to be in. And while we were there surrounded by dozens of kids, I said, 'I wanted to have your children once.' "

"That was cruel, wasn't it?"

"Unconscionably cruel and the worst part is that I knew it. I said it to hurt him, and I knew it would hurt. And he responded . . . not very well."

"I can imagine."

"When I was 17, I decided what sort of life I wanted and that life didn't include having children. But if that's what he wanted, if what's in that photograph was something he dreamed of, something he desired, he should have told me. He had a thousand chances to tell me, to ask me, to share his heart with me. You know what it is? It's not jealousy right here." She tapped her breast again. "It's anger. I am angry at him for not telling me how much he wanted that. He should have told me. Even if it meant putting our relationship through another trial, he should have told me. I'm furious at him for not trusting that our love was strong enough to go through that together. That's what hurts. That's why it stings. Because I wanted to know that. Because that's a beautiful thing, isn't it? That there's this part of him that desires fatherhood and to sit in a chair in front of the mother of his child and watch while she nurses their son? That's nothing to be ashamed of, nothing to be embarrassed about. That's something special, something beautiful. It's a diamond in his heart, and he kept that diamond hidden from me. And he shouldn't have kept it hidden. He didn't have to give me that diamond. He just had to show it to me. Because it's so . . . fucking . . . sweet. Isn't it?"

Her tears came then, big ones to wet the shoulder of his cassock all the way to his skin. Stuart held her against him, her arms around his neck and her head on his arm. And she cried like a baby and he rocked her like a baby because she was a baby. God's child, right here in his arms. God's little girl. "The Lord is close to the brokenhearted." Psalm 38. And here was a brokenhearted child of God right in his arms. What a blessing to be a priest with tenderhearted sinners like this in the world.

"It's very sweet," he whispered. "Maybe that's why he didn't tell you about it. He's not a very sweet man, is he? A real arsehole most of the time."

She shuddered in his arms with tears and laughter.

"Can't stand him myself," Stuart continued. "Big blond brute strutting around with all his height and his massive brain and his handsome face—and he's getting too old to still be that handsome. You better believe I resent the hell out of it."

"Tell me about it," she groaned. "He's prettier now than he was twenty years ago. I hate him."

"Oh, and there's that look he gives you. You know the look. The magnifying glass in the sunlight look, and you're there on the sidewalk like an ant burnt to a crisp."

"I know that look," she said between ragged breaths. "I've been that toasted ant more than once."

"He gets off on it, you know," Ballard said. "Gets off on seeming scary and tough. And all this time he had a gooey secret marshmallow in his heart. He was probably too embarrassed to tell you about it. You might think he'd gone soft. No man wants to go soft in front of his lover."

"Oh no, not soft. Anything but that."

"You're allowed to be hurt that he kept a side of himself from you. So many men keep secrets from their wives and lovers—drinking habits, drugs, gambling, cheating. That makes sense, keeping the bad stuff a secret. But he kept the good stuff a secret from you. I think that would hurt worse. I think that would hurt the most."

"It does hurt the most. I know all his darkness. I could carry that. I could handle all the bad stuff and the hard stuff and the scary stuff he's told me. And here was this one beautiful shining secret part of him, and that's the part he kept from me? It's not fair. We aren't sweet people, Father. Not me, not Kingsley, not Søren. We're a lot of things but we aren't sweet. And all along he had this sweet fantasy, this lovely longing for something like a teenage girl imagining her wedding day, and he never shared that with me."

"Even when he's sweet he still manages to be a bastard somehow. You ought to cane him. I hear you're good at it."

"The best in the business."

"You know there are two things you have to consider here, Eleanor," he said, patting the back of her head. "First of all, maybe he didn't know he had that diamond, as you call it, until he had his son. I've known many a man who swore up and down he didn't want children until he became a father. Then overnight he becomes a new man. You're imagining he kept a secret from you. You have to admit he might not have known the secret himself. The heart's a labyrinth, even our own hearts, even to us."

"I hadn't considered that."

"You also have to consider that the reason Marcus never told you about his desire to have children wasn't because he knew you'd say no. There's a good chance he didn't ask you because he thought maybe . . . maybe you would say yes."

She sat up and looked at him. "He thought I might say yes?"

"It's not out of the realm of possibility for a woman in love with a man to change her mind about having children. It happens all the time. And what would have happened if you'd agreed to have his child? What would he have done?"

"He would have left the priesthood," she said. "The day I told him I was pregnant, he would have called the bishop."

"Of course he would have."

"He doesn't want to leave the priesthood or the Jesuits. He's never wanted to leave."

Ballard nodded. "Whether he wants to admit it or not, Marcus is a human being. And human beings often want things they can't have. A man wants to lose weight, but he also wants to eat ice cream. A woman who wants to marry also wants to run from relationships because she's afraid of turning into her mother. A man who wants to be a priest also wants to marry and have children—"

"He did have a child."

"With a married woman. He wouldn't leave the Church to marry a woman who was already married. No reason to leave the Church, right?"

"After we found out about Fionn, after Zach told us, I asked Søren about that night with Grace and what happened. All he said was, 'Little One, please believe me, I was meant to do this.' And I believed him. When I held Fionn in my arms I knew it was true. He was meant to be that boy's father. Why, I don't know and I don't care. But he was."

"I'm old school where children are concerned," Ballard said. "I think every child is part of God's plan. But maybe this little boy—this miracle as you call him—maybe he's a very special part of the plan."

A fresh tear ran down her cheek. She started to wipe it away with the back of her hand, and he handed her a tissue from his stash.

"Thank you," she said, dabbing her eyes, once more the duchess, no more the troubled teenaged girl.

"You're welcome. We all need a good cry every now and then. I had one myself just this morning."

"Did you stub your soul too?"

"I looked in the mirror without bracing myself."

"Hush, you're very handsome."

"What did I say about flirting with me?"

"Sorry, sorry." She held the tissue in her hand. Her eyes were bright green, incandescent from her tears. "He did it to protect me. That's all."

"That's all it is," Stuart said. "But you can still be hurt by it. You should forgive him, though. His intentions were good."

"They were. They always are where I'm concerned. I'll forgive him, I promise. Once I get up the courage to confess to him I looked through his Bible."

"Good luck with that. He still scares the shite out of me."

"Oh, no, he doesn't."

"He doesn't, but don't tell him that. It'll hurt his little feelings."

"You're a very good priest," she said. "I'm glad we finally got to meet. He speaks very highly of you."

"Not so fast. You still haven't given me a real sin yet. I can't wrap this thing up until you do. It's not until I've absolved and reconciled you."

"We went over everything. I have committed no mortal sins."

"Make something up then!"

"Um . . ." She held up her hands. "Come on, Nora, you make up stuff for a living. Wait. I got it. Daniel Craig."

"The actor?"

"Yes, him. James Bond. He's married."

"He is."

"I want to fuck him."

"Well, who doesn't? He shows up in half the confessions I hear."

"Doesn't Jesus say that if you look upon someone and lust after them in your heart, you've committed adultery?"

"He does, yes. But we're fairly certain lust means you'd do it if given the opportunity. Simple sexual attraction doesn't count as lust."

"It's not simple sexual attraction. I'd steal him from his wife, and we'd run away to Italy and live together in a crumbling Tuscan palazzo, and we'd leave the world behind, and it would be nothing but wine and food and sex until we ate ourselves, drank ourselves, and fucked ourselves to death. Now that's lust. But more importantly, it's adultery."

"That *is* adultery. Excellent. Well done."

"So you can absolve me?"

"I will the second you tell me who we're really talking about." He raised his eyebrows at her and waited.

"You're good," she said. "Very good."

"I've had a lot of practice seeing through masks. Take off yours."

"Zach," she said with a heavy sigh. "Grace's husband. My editor. I still have feelings for him. Very strong feelings that make me tempted to do things I shouldn't do."

"You and Marcus have a complicated relationship with this couple, don't you?"

"Understatement of the century. And it doesn't help that I traded Grace a night with Søren for a week with Zach. She ended up with a child. I ended up with a . . . I don't know, a dream of what could have been. And the man is ridiculously so good at anal."

"Eleanor."

"An ass-master, I swear. He's better than Nico and Søren and they're both fantastic. Every night for a week. I couldn't walk, but I was happy."

"You're trying to give me a heart attack. That's not nice."

"Sorry. Sorry." She raised her hands in surrender. "I had to get that out."

"I think you keep as many secrets from him as he keeps from you."

"Yeah, but I only keep the secrets that would . . ."

"Hurt his little feelings?" Stuart finished her thought for her.

"Damn, you *are* a good priest."

He blew on his nails and brushed them on his cassock. That got another laugh at her.

"Father, I love Søren and Nico. I'm in love with them. I don't want to feel this way about someone else. What do I do?"

"First you have to see your feelings for what they are, not what you think they are. What happened that week with Zach that sticks with you? And not the . . . you know."

"The sex," she said.

"That. You said that week with this Zach gentleman left you with 'a dream of what could have been.' What's that dream?"

"That week is the week I met Nico. It was right after we found out about Fionn. That week with Zach in France was the last . . . I don't know, the last easy week of my life."

"Easy? How so?"

"When I met Nico, he fell in lust with me. Has a thing for older women."

"I used to. Then I turned 81. Now I can't find any older women. But tell your boy I approve of his tastes."

"I absolutely will. Anyway . . . Kingsley's son, Nico. That was hard after meeting him, knowing that he was going to complicate my life. Complicate it even more. Wes made things difficult, but at least we lived on the same continent. That week with Zach was the last week before everything changed. I keep going back to it in my mind, living there, wishing we'd had more time, wishing I could stop time and stay in France longer. Not forever. Forever belongs to Søren. Just longer. I love my life but it's not easy being in love with two men in two different counties. Why couldn't Nico have been Canadian or Mexican? He had to be French? Really? So unfair."

"I suppose I don't have to tell you, of all people, that life isn't fair?"

"Nope," she said.

"You say that was the last week before everything changed, before everything got harder. Isn't it possible that what you're lusting for is not the man but the life you were living before meeting Nico? That and . . ." He punched the air and she nodded. She caught his drift. "By your own choosing, you have two lovers and one of your lovers has another lover of his own *and* a child. You enjoy that life. You chose that life. But you know better than I do that it's a hard life, " he said. "You're not merely lusting after a married man. You're lusting for a life you can't have—a simple life. *Simpler,* anyway."

"That's a big part of it. Maybe the biggest part."

"The great heartache of my life was discovering this truth— there is no such thing as a simple life. We all want it, all seek it. It doesn't exist, Eleanor. Not on this side of Heaven. I'm a man without a wife, without children. I don't pay my own bills, I have a guaranteed roof over my head until my dying breath. I have my health and nothing to worry about, and even I don't lead a simple life. You can't have a simple life with a wild heart like yours. The simple life is a mirage. It's like a perfectly clean and polished wine glass. And you want that pristine chalice, but the second you reach out and pick it up, it's covered in your fingerprints. It's only clean until it's yours, then it's dirty. That's the simple life. It's simple until you show up and start using it."

"I know you're right," she said. "But the desire's still there. Such a beautiful mirage. It's hard not to look at it when I'm on the plane to France leaving Søren and America behind, and I know I only have four weeks with Nico before I'm back again. And I already miss Søren and I already miss Nico."

"Steal him then. Your Zach. If you tried, could you steal him?"

"I'm Nora Fucking Sutherlin. You bet your ass I could."

Stuart laughed. He did love a woman with moxie.

"What's stopping you then?" he asked.

"My conscience?"

"You sure about that?"

"No."

"What's stopping you then?" he repeated, more slowly this time, letting the words hit her one at a time.

"Because I'd have to give up Nico and Søren."

"And you don't want to."

"No. I don't want to. My life is harder. But it's better," she said. "So much better than it was before. . . ."

"There's your answer."

"And yet the fantasy remains."

"Well, I still fantasize sometimes about getting married and having babies, and I'm 81 and a Jesuit. Wonder if Marcus ever has that fantasy? The simple life?"

"I'm sure he does," Eleanor said.

"I'm sure he does, too. You think that's what that photograph is? A small glimpse into his dream of a simpler life?"

"I'm sure it is," she said. "But he wouldn't choose it anymore than I would. And yet you still dream. . . ."

"Exactly. Human nature," Ballard said.

"What are you going to do?"

The question was rhetorical. He answered it anyway.

"I'm going to absolve you, dear girl. That's what I'm going to do."

"Finally." She held up her hand, and he slapped it in a high five. "Absolve me good and hard, Father Ballard. This adulterous harlot needs it."

"You promise you feel contrite about your sinful urges?"

"I do. I really do. I'm trying to be a good girl these days. My only two lovers are Søren and Nico. No more married guys, especially not ones raising small children. No more drama. I fuck a priest and I fuck my priest's lover's son and that's as drama-free as this bitch gets."

"This is the strangest confession I've ever heard in my life, and that includes all of Marcus's various and sundry perversions."

She winked at him. "You're welcome."

"Any other sins we've missed? Anything you didn't confess to Marcus?"

"I got Dairy Queen on Ash Wednesday."

"Now that's a mortal sin if I've ever heard one. Go on. Say your Act of Contrition. . . ."

"Lord God, I am sorry for my sins. I am. I have sinned against you and against your Church. Forgive me for my sins and lead me with your grace and love."

"God the Father of mercies, through the death and resurrection of your son, you have reconciled the world to yourself and sent the Holy Spirit among us for the forgiveness of sins. May God grant you pardon and peace. And I absolve you of your sins, in the name of the Father, and of the Son and of the Holy Spirit," he said as he made the sign of the cross in front of her and she crossed herself accordingly. "Amen."

"Amen."

"Feel better?" he asked.

"I like the prayer of absolution better in Latin."

"Out of my confessional, you bewitching temptress. And give me my Jolly Rancher back. Cherry is my favorite."

She popped it in her mouth.

"Jezebel," he said, shaking his head.

"Thank you, Father." She held out her hand to shake and instead he kissed the back of it as gallantly as an old man with a touch of palsy was able.

"You're good for him, and I'm glad he has you," he whispered. "But don't ever tell anyone I said that."

She gave him a tiny smile. "Our little secret," she whispered.

She started for the door and then stopped. "Wait. Penance. Are you giving me any penance?"

"Penance? You? His lover? My dear Eleanor—you love a priest. The sin itself carries its own penance."

She laughed and it was such a laugh he knew her soul was healed.

"Shouldn't you at least tell me to go forth and sin no more?" she asked, leaning in to hug him goodbye.

"Why on earth would I do that?" he asked, wrapping his arms around her and enjoying the feel of a beautiful woman's body against his. No sin there. And if there was, it was only venial. "This is the most fun I've had in years."

THE CONFESSION OF
TIFFANY REISZ

This conversation was conducted by book reviewer Cyndy Aleo on January 22, 2016 via Skype chat. It has been edited for clarity, errors, and length. Insertions and explanations of terminology and abbreviations are in brackets.

TIFFANY: Hello? Is it me you're looking for?

CYNDY: Hello from the other side.

TIFFANY: Hello! How are you? That's not a song, by the way, just a real question.

CYNDY: LOL. Good! How are you?

TIFFANY: Very good. Can you introduce yourself to the readers?

CYNDY: Lapsed book reviewer, lapsed Catholic, Tiffany acolyte?

TIFFANY: Perfect! [Cyndy is possibly the biggest fan of *The Angel* on the planet.] I'm ready when you are!

CYNDY: READY.

TIFFANY: HIT ME.

CYNDY: So the first topic I wanted to talk about is Søren's kinks.

TIFFANY: He would say, "Kink. Singular." He might be kidding himself.

CYNDY: Pretty much every book with Nora and Søren together has made me light-headed at some point, even when it's felt like you were working down my personal [kinky] checklist.

TIFFANY: Bad lightheaded, I assume? As in I crossed a boundary with you?

CYNDY: How do you figure out where to draw that line with him each time? How does HE? With Nora [that is]. We know there isn't really a line with King—more of a guideline.

TIFFANY: I wish I could say I was really thoughtful and contemplative when writing kink scenes, but usually all I'm doing is getting into that character's head and doing what I think they'd enjoy. So if the character isn't worried about crossing a line, then I'm not either.

CYNDY: Obviously I'm not vanilla, and GOD KNOWS I have read some filthy things . . . but you really take things to an edge. For instance, in *The Queen*, the first Nora/Søren scene is Daddy Kink in a D/s relationship where Søren—both in the novels and in some reader response—has been occasionally accused of "grooming." That is right the hell to the edge with pin-wheeling arms.

TIFFANY: I'm picturing your arms pin-wheeling and it's amusing me very much.

With Søren, I've never written in his point of view so I can't speak as authoritatively as I can with other characters . . . but he is a man who understands pain AND suffering. I think his line is, "Pain, but not suffering."

The Daddy Kink scene in *The Queen* exists because A) I always wanted to write [Daddy play] and B) I know Nora would enjoy doing it. And if Nora would enjoy it, Søren would want to do that with her and for her. The same way you give your partner a back rub for your partner and not for you. So yeah, you enjoy making your partner feel good but it's your partner getting the back rub, not you. So the Daddy play scene was Søren rubbing Nora's, um . . . back.

Yeah, let's go with back.

One other thing that happens when I write is that if my brain starts to light up and I start to write REALLY REALLY fast I know I'm onto something. I know it'll freak out some readers (mainly my husband) but other readers will LOVE it. And I'd rather get a strong love AND hate response than a tepid "that was nice" response.

CYNDY: A three-star review is death. You never want meh.

TIFFANY: Never ever. Better a one-star review. I've sold a lot of books because of some one-star reviews of *The Siren*.

CYNDY: So [getting back to grooming] you really don't think, for instance, "Hey, this is a character who's been accused of ephebophilia [sexual interest in mid- to late-adolescents] by both a character or two as well as a reader or two? Maaaaaybe the Daddy Kink is taking it a bit too far?"

TIFFANY: Nah. I probably SHOULD think about that stuff but I don't. The thing is that I write for adults and what I write for adults is the "forbidden love" trope. Classic trope. Goes back to the beginning of literature. Lancelot and Queen Guinevere were a forbidden-love trope story. So if you write forbidden love and you read forbidden love you're going to get characters doing things they absolutely should not do in the real world. Fun to read? Yes. Fun to experience in real life? Probably not.

CYNDY: So in that light, do you ever think you HAVE gone too far? Does your editor ever say something like, "OMG, Tiffany, this King/Søren scene in *The Prince* is seriously dub-con [dubious consent] and this is Not Okay."

TIFFANY: I'm trying to think if I ever thought I went too far? Hmmm . . . I wish I could say yes. But my editor has pulled me back a time or two. And usually it's the stuff I never thought would bother her that bothers her. Example: I had a tiny little bit of snowballing in *The Prince* and she was like NO! SAFE WORD! CUT! (To readers who do not know what snowballing is, it's when Partner A ejaculates into the mouth of Partner B and then Partner B kisses Partner A and gives Partner A their semen back.)

CYNDY: OMG, really?

TIFFANY: And I did because she usually lets me get away with murder.

CYNDY: If you saved that scene, feel free to email it to me . . . for science.

TIFFANY: [But] there is dubious consent in *The Prince* in those scenes that take place in the past. No denying it. But I like reading dub-con and I like writing it and my readers are (or should be) adults. And I do believe two very troubled teenaged boys who are exploring their kinks under those circumstances [at an all boys school in the middle of nowhere isolated from friends and family] would cross boundaries with each other. You try to achieve psychological accuracy and believability with fictional characters and often it's not very pretty.

CYNDY: I think that's what's always drawn me to your books. You walk that tightrope SO well of, "Okay, this is seriously going right to the point of where I'd DNF [Did Not Finish]" but it just puts, like, a toenail on that line.

TIFFANY: I love straddling the line. It's where art lives. And people love having their buttons pushed. That's why we ride roller coasters.

CYNDY: The scenes I think I was closest to having to put the books down are that [dub-con] scene in *The Prince* and, yes, the Daddy Kink. Where I'm saying out loud as I'm reading, "No, she's not. She's not . . . OMG, she is."

TIFFANY: SHE IS. My editor DID NOT like the Daddy Kink scene in *The Queen* and I fought for it. Glad I did though because I had a lot of great reactions to it from readers. When one reader tells you that you wrote her most forbidden fantasy and a reviewer says, "I get Daddy play now and I never did before," then I felt like I made the right choice. And honestly, I thought that scene was so freaking hot to write. TMI? Don't care.

CYNDY: Which is what makes this series so amazing. Like, after *The Siren*, I remember our mutual friend [name redacted] going, "But you don't read [this type of stuff] . . . or this . . . or this. . . ." and me saying I KNOW BUT YOU HAVE TO [READ THIS].

TIFFANY: Thank you! I love when readers read despite themselves. Like I do NOT read World War II books so if you catch me reading one, you know it's amazing.

CYNDY: Because it does walk that line, and the reactions of the characters to the scenes are so authentic and the fallout of those to-the-edge scenes . . . I have no words. Ever.

TIFFANY: I try. It helps that I'm kinky and I'm a Switch so I have felt what they've all felt at one point or another.

I love moral conundrums. One came up recently after the great David Bowie died. A woman wrote a blog post about how she lost her virginity to David Bowie in the '70s when she was about 14 or 15, and she loved the experience and considers it a very positive experience.

CYNDY: OMG. I missed that post. I think I'm glad I did.

TIFFANY: What do we do when someone says they enjoyed and consented to something society and the law says they cannot enjoy and cannot consent to? We say a 15-year-old girl doesn't have the sexual agency to consent to sex with an adult man but now she is an adult woman and says she was not sexually assaulted and considers it a good experience. Do we take her agency away from her as an adult woman by telling her what she feels and believes is wrong?

I don't know the answer. That's why I write these books. Not because I want to know the answer, but because I want to explore the question.

CYNDY: Which was why I DID recommend *The Siren* to so many people even with so many of the usual things I don't read.

Are some kids at 15 okay to have a relationship with adults? Probably. But we legislate because we can't assume maturity levels at a given age.

TIFFANY: Just a note to readers: All my books are beta read by women with teenage children. (A beta reader is someone, usually another professional author, who reads a book before it gets published and gives the author feedback.) So all the sex in the book is run by an actual parent of actual teenagers. Not that that makes it okay, just saying I do get a parental POV before I publish anything [that includes teenagers].

CYNDY: And Michael was a unique case.

TIFFANY: EXACTLY. And let me pause and just go . . . Mick! I love that kid. Anywho, back to the discussion.

CYNDY: The character who's always been bigger for me in the books than even Søren. . . . (Cyndy waits while Tiffany blinks and wonders where she's going.)

TIFFANY: Where are you going, Cyndy?

CYNDY: The Church.

TIFFANY: A-ha! The Roman Catholic Church. Yup, there is no Original Sinners [series] without the Church.

CYNDY: So, Søren (like you) is a convert. Mick and Nora are cradle Catholics, with Mick originally let down by the Church, and Nora returning to the Church. And then Kingsley has an adversarial relationship the entire time with Catholicism. ["Cradle Catholic" refers to someone born to Catholic parents, raised in the Catholic Church who likely also attended Catholic schools.

Tiffany is an adult convert to the Roman Catholic Church, not a cradle Catholic.] For starters, how much does Søren's faith journey parallel your own?

TIFFANY: Søren's faith journey is something I really want to explore more. I've written ABOUT it, but I haven't written IT yet. Although I want to.

Side note, I've talked to my editor about writing a book with 14-year-old Søren converting [to Catholicism] and deciding to become a priest, and she said she'd love to read that. But back to the convo here. . . .

My faith journey is nothing like Søren's. Luckily he and I have almost nothing in common. I had a good childhood for example and the Catholic Church was my father's church and my grandparents'. It just wasn't my mom's, ergo I didn't go to the Catholic Church growing up. I became a Christian in college and then read a lot of Philip Yancey who turned me on to G.K. Chesterton who turned me Catholic. Chesterton will do that. So Catholicism was an intellectual journey for me and a way of me connecting with my father's family.

Meanwhile Søren . . . he was adrift on a dangerous sea and the Jesuits were his lifeboat.

CYNDY: And yet you were in a Protestant seminary and then went to Catholicism. . . .

TIFFANY: Right. I went to a Methodist seminary and while there I did more reading of the Church Fathers, etc., and really felt that eventually I would convert to Catholicism. And I did. I was 32, I think . . . ? Søren was 14. So very different journeys.

CYNDY: Is it the same kind of thing for Søren as a problem child heading off to boot camp and becoming a career officer? Jesuits are pretty hardcore.

TIFFANY: I think that's a great analogy. Jesuits are known as "God's Army" and "God's Marines" and "God's soldiers." I'm 99 percent certain the discipline along with the caring combined to make joining their ranks very attractive to him.

Also, his father shit a brick when he did it and God knows that was probably a big deciding factor too. Not even Søren is immune to the desire to rebel against a parent.

CYNDY: And yet you gave all these other characters so many different ways of interacting with and feeling about the Church. How much of a conscious decision was that?

TIFFANY: It would have been intellectually dishonest if I hadn't done that. First of all, there are GREAT reasons to hate the Catholic Church. I've dated too many atheists and agnostics to pretend those reasons don't exist. And I know too much about the sexual abuse in the clergy to ignore those reasons.

CYNDY: That was so key.

TIFFANY: So it was a very conscious decision to include detractors of the Catholic Church. And I've been there. I probably would have called myself an agnostic in high school. Any big huge group of men telling people, especially women, how to behave will raise my hackles.

CYNDY: And honestly, at least in my experience, there has always been a chasm between cradle Catholics and converts, yet you seemed to develop these characters who totally GOT the issues those of us who left have, and those of us who have questioned.

TIFFANY: That's the great fun of being a writer, is getting to crawl inside the souls of so many different people, people I may have nothing in common with.

CYNDY: Which is so ironic to me, because high school was when I was thumping my Bible and quoting Scripture.

TIFFANY: And here I am a churchgoer and you quit the Church (for very good reasons, I might add). We are proof God has a sense of humor. I'll believe that to my dying day.

CYNDY: I think that was what drew me so much to King—he hates the Church. For more than just taking Søren from him?

TIFFANY: King hates the Church for a lot of reasons. He's a rebel. Born rebel. Don't tell him what to do. Don't tell him how to behave. He hates politicians too. Anyone who moralizes will get the stink-eye from King.

And he's of the "what a waste" school of thought when it comes to Søren. It's like when you hear someone has gone gluten-free and you know they don't have Celiac and you're like, "Why are you torturing yourself by giving up bread FOR NO GOOD REASON?" That's how King feels about vows of celibacy.

Of course my own private theology is responsible for the very different relationships every character has to God. And that's the theology that's not so private anymore because I gave it to Nora in *The Saint* when she talks about how God is a writer and we are His characters.

CYNDY: And I agree on the vows of celibacy, but I also agree with Nora (and OMG, you are so great at segueing very neatly into my topics here): Søren isn't Søren unless he's a priest. If there's a devil and an angel on Søren's shoulders in that regard, they are Nora and King.

TIFFANY: Kingsley doesn't believe in God really. Well, Kingsley also doesn't believe in me. He doesn't know I exist. But I love him.

CYNDY: And their relationships [with Søren] are two sides of a coin. How hard was it to build them [Nora and Kingsley] to be so alike and yet so different?

TIFFANY: Søren is not Søren unless he's a priest. Which is why I didn't just have him quit the priesthood. There goes the drama. There goes Søren. He is a man born to walk the knife's edge, not the handle, not the flat part of the blade. The edge.

CYNDY: For instance, Søren/Nora are what we'd view as pretty much traditional D/s with a sadist who only goes to a point with her . . . but Søren/King is walking that very, very sharp edge we talked about earlier.

TIFFANY: Kingsley was not originally intended to be as important a character as he turned into. He started stealing scenes in *The Angel*. Then he stole all of *The Prince*.

CYNDY: I remain convinced you had this entire thing written in your head before you wrote your first line.

TIFFANY: You can believe that. I want you to believe that. I think we all have people in our lives who bring out the best in us and those who bring out the worst in us. And it's scary how drawn we are to those who bring out the worst in us.

For Søren, his best is him being a responsible, caring and CAREFUL sadist. His worst is being the sadist he would be if it were suddenly proved the heavens were empty and there is no God. When he's with Nora, God's watching. When he's with King, God is not looking. Or at least Søren hopes God isn't looking. Hence the "God closed his eyes" line in *The Prince*.

CYNDY: OOOH. I love that analogy. I'm using that to explain my dating history, BTW ("how drawn we are to those who bring out the worst in us . . .").

TIFFANY: What changes with Søren and Kingsley in the series, and why they ultimately start sleeping together again, is because Kingsley learns boundaries for himself. When he knows he's finally going to be a father, and Nora tells him to start taking care of himself [in *The Mistress*] it finally sinks in with Kingsley. God comes into the relationship with him and Søren. It's not a free-for-all anymore. Consequences exist again. Søren can play safely with Kingsley now because Kingsley has boundaries where before he didn't.

Someone thought I was being unfair to Kingsley by making him wait so many years for him and Søren to reconcile. But Kingsley was being a little unfair to Søren by pushing Søren to do things Søren didn't want to do. CORRECTION: Søren wanted to do them but he didn't want to want to do them.

CYNDY: The other thing I liked about them is that I think it explained to a lot of readers what RACK was. After That Certain Book [*Fifty Shades of Grey*], there was a lot of confusion about RACK vs. SSC and an insistence that SSC was the only way.

TIFFANY: For confused readers, SSC means "safe, sane, and consensual" and RACK means "Risk-Aware Consensual Kink." [These are two different philosophies/attitudes toward BDSM play.] The Original Sinners do RACK. RACK adherents accept that you can't always be safe.

CYNDY: Do you think it was an unconscious decision on your part to show the difference [between RACK and SSC]?

TIFFANY: I think it was fairly conscious because I sympathize more with RACK myself than SSC. Not that there's anything wrong with SSC. But if you're the kind of person who likes bloodplay there's not really an SSC way to do bloodplay. The skin will be broken. There will be blood.

I wish *There Will Be Blood* had been about actual blood and not oil.

CYNDY: *The Prince* [explored the theme] "here's where RACK can go awry."

TIFFANY: Exactly. *The Prince* is not a "how to" guide. It's more of a "how not to" guide. Actually it's just a story, a forbidden love story. But we hear horror stories all the time in the news about teenage boys engaging in shocking acts of violence toward girls and often toward each other. At that age, part of the brain that understands consequences and empathy is [temporarily] shut down for construction. This is not an ideal state for engaging in BDSM.

CYNDY: And here we are back to teens having sex and agency. . . . I think it meant a lot to have THAT (the Søren/King scene in *The Prince*) AFTER the scene with Nora/Mick in *The Siren*.

TIFFANY: And I don't know the answer. Again, it's the questions that matter more to me. Mainly because the answer is different for everyone.

CYNDY: Because each is an individual circumstance.

TIFFANY: Right. And Nora and Mick in *The Siren* is a moment of profound healing for Michael. Did it make people uncomfortable? Well, sure. But did it make Michael better? Yeah. In this fictional world it did. Michael had been through more at age 15 than I had by age 30.

CYNDY: I also think a lot has changed for kids in terms of discussing sexual agency and identity than when Søren and King were teens. Mick has had a completely different era to grow up in. I didn't know what BDSM was at 16.

TIFFANY: Yes, I had to remind someone recently that Kingsley and Søren were born in the mid-'60s. They are both over 50 now (or would be if they existed). If you watch movies from the '70s you'll see Jodie Foster AND Brooke Shields both playing prostitutes in movies. And they were about 12 at the time. Brooke Shields even had a nude scene in the movie *Pretty Baby* when she was 12 or 13. That would not happen today.

CYNDY: Brooke Shields was nude a LOT back then. Way before she was 18.

TIFFANY: True! Brooke, God bless her.

CYNDY: And we've talked about this, but my first experience [with BDSM] was more or less having it thrown in front of me and being absolutely horrified that people did this to each other.

It took a lot more soul searching to get to a point where it was like "OMG, this is something it's okay to talk about."

TIFFANY: As for Nora and Michael, Nora's basically a sex surrogate in that scene in *The Siren*, a sex therapist. A teenager recovering from a suicide attempt caused by pain over his sexuality, a sex therapist might be good for him. I won't say, "It's good Nora fucked him." I will say that Michael would say, "I don't care if YOU think it's right or wrong, but I needed it."

CYNDY: Yes. And I never at any point thought he wasn't in a place where he could give consent. Fully informed and very enthusiastic consent.

TIFFANY: I was in the car with my cousin when she was about 15 and we were talking about sex. I said, "Sex is fun." And she said, "You're the first adult who ever told me sex was fun." That breaks my heart.

CYNDY: If anything, the dub-con there [in *The Siren*] was with Nora, who didn't have the whole story.

TIFFANY: And again, you are a parent of teenagers and so was at least one of my beta readers. Søren deserved a huge slap in the face for that [dub-con scene]. But that was a dark time for him. To say the least.

CYNDY: What's so funny to me is that my kids are so much less obsessed with [sex] than I think I was. We were all reading *Clan of the Cave Bear* for the dirty parts. My kids are like, "Will you please never explain an Angry Dragon again? We're sorry we asked."

TIFFANY: I've noticed that too.

CYNDY: But speaking of kids . . .

TIFFANY: Yes . . .

CYNDY: I did not message you with my nearly automatic swears when I was reading *The Queen*. But you sort of backgrounded the Søren/Fionn meeting.

TIFFANY: I did. I'm evil like that. I just needed that to be in Nora's POV and I needed to let Kingsley have THAT moment with Søren.

CYNDY: That was a "Here's Jesus at 12. You won't see him again for 20 years or so" moment. [This refers to The Gospel According Luke 2:41-53 in which Jesus at age 12 runs away from his parents and is found in the Jerusalem Temple listening to the teachers and asking intelligent questions of them far beyond his years. Readers don't see Jesus again in the Gospel accounts of his life until he begins his public ministry at about age 30-32.] And if Søren is God . . .

TIFFANY: Nora is giving Kingsley THE WORLD right then, by letting him introduce Fionn to Søren. And yeah, it is kind of a Jesus in the Temple at 12 moment . . . so Fionn . . . I'm dying to write Fionn books. DYING.

But they are still percolating.

90% sure he ends up in the Vienna Boys Choir.

CYNDY: Is he the Messiah, Tiffany?

TIFFANY: I don't know! I want to know more about Fionn. I have to write the books to know who he is.

He could be the anti-Christ.

CYNDY: My face right now. . . . I was just explaining the castrati to my 12-year-old, who has a beautiful soprano.

TIFFANY: Give him [Anne Rice's] *Cry to Heaven* to read.

CYNDY: [cackles] But seriously . . . how much of that was intentional? I mean, we have God insemination . . . we have the very patient husband who is pretty much okay that his wife shows up pregnant by some miracle. . . .

TIFFANY: Grace having Søren's baby was 100% the Messiah story.

TIFFANY: Grace/Mary. Zach (who is Jewish, remember?)/ Joseph. Søren/God the Father.

CYNDY: Not going to lie here . . . I'm sort of hoping Fionn is the Messiah of this motley group of characters you've written. But more along the line of Reza Aslan's Jesus than the Christian version.

TIFFANY: Yeah, I had too much fun with that. And I love Grace. Just love her. Soon as I started writing her I was wild about her. It was such a joy writing Søren through her eyes. This pure faith she has in him. She just gets him.

I still need to read Reza's book. But speaking of Aslan [joke], also entirely intentional was the "walking at dawn" scene in *The Mistress*. In *The Lion, The Witch, and The Wardrobe*, Lucy and Susan walk with Aslan to his certain death. They keep him company and comfort him in his darkest hour. Grace got to be Søren's Lucy.

And Fionn is special. I can't wait to see what he turns into. I know he and Celeste have a very special relationship. They won't be a romantic couple because that's too obvious. Maybe more like Jesus and John, the beloved disciple.

CYNDY: John ends up with his head on a plate.

TIFFANY: That's John the Baptist.

CYNDY: Oh . . . you're thinking John the disciple.

TIFFANY: John the Disciple. The one disciple who wasn't martyred. We think. History is murky.

CYNDY: I was thinking you meant John the Baptist. Especially with that later in life, second-chance thing. And they were born around the same time. . . .

TIFFANY: I'm sure I'll have a John the Baptist if I ever write more of the series. I'd like to but we have to pray my publisher will want them. *fingers crossed*

CYNDY: So on that note . . .

TIFFANY: True. I could run with that. But I don't want to chop Celeste's head off.

CYNDY: You've alluded to a possible Søren conversion story, possible Fionn books. . . .

TIFFANY: I have! Yes.

CYNDY: . . . I need to know about possible King stuff.

TIFFANY: Ohhhhh . . . King. Hmm . . . good question. I had a reader demand a book about Kingsley when he was working as a spy for France. I do not want to write that.

CYNDY: YES.

TIFFANY: NO. That is too much research.

CYNDY: I have here in my notes "Ask about FFL [French Foreign Legion] King."

TIFFANY: You just like it when King is shooting his gun.

CYNDY: Because just King fucking his way across the desert a la *Lawrence of Arabia* would seriously do it for me.

TIFFANY: I'm 100% certain I'll write a Kingsley-centric Original Sinners Christmas novella someday.

CYNDY: I do like when King is shooting his gun. In all respects.

TIFFANY: I'll add that to the idea file.

CYNDY: (sighs) Young Peter O'Toole.

TIFFANY: The thing is . . . the Sinners are at their best when they're with each other. Keeping them apart in *The Virgin* was so hard to write. That was the hardest of all the books to write because the three of them were estranged from each other.

Every scene is more electric when you put two of the UnHoly Trinity in the same room. At least the writing is more electric if not the reading.

CYNDY: I dunno. Sam is one of my favorite characters.

TIFFANY: God, I love Sam too. She's my dream girl.

CYNDY: And that was just King and Sam for most of that.

TIFFANY: BUT even in *The King* and loving Sam, my favorite scenes are still the ones between King and Søren.

CYNDY: Always.

TIFFANY: When King calls Søren in the middle of the night and tempts Søren with sex? Favorite scene to write. That and the baptism scene in the swimming pool.

CYNDY: But I would read a Sam/King road trip book, too.

TIFFANY: That could be fun. I do want to put all the Sinners on a train. Sort of like [Agatha Christie's] *Murder on the Orient Express* but with fucking instead of murder?

CYNDY: If you put them all on a train there WOULD be murder.

TIFFANY: That is a good point. As to the future of the Original Sinners . . . I would LOVE to write more books but not for a few years. I need the break. Also we'll have to figure out the logistics. If my publisher doesn't want to buy more, that makes it much harder for me to write and publish them. But I'm keeping my hopes up.

CYNDY: They need their extracurriculars to keep them from killing each other. And speaking of . . . what's up with Nico?

TIFFANY: Nico! Nico was born of necessity. I needed Nora to have SOMEONE to tell the story of her and Søren to and that someone had to be A) invested in that story in some way and B) hadn't already heard the story. And my editor said *The Saint* needed more sex so it had to be someone Nora would fuck. Ergo . . . Nico.

Plus it was about time Nora got the male sub she'd been aching for all her life.

CYNDY: Worth a note to readers about the reality of series drop-off and how important it is to KEEP BUYING THE DAMN BOOKS!

TIFFANY: True. If all the Original Sinners books hit the *New York Times* bestseller list (none of them did), then I could write them forever. As they didn't, there may not be more full-length books. But I will at least continue to write the Christmas stories and other random stories time permitting.

CYNDY: If even the LAST one did . . . (I can shill here, folks, so Tiffany doesn't have to.)

TIFFANY: I could write Søren forever, though. I just hope I can. I do have bills to pay.

You're a wonderful pimp, Cyndy.

CYNDY: I prefer to think of it as a hype man.

TIFFANY: Word.

I do need to write at least one more book so I can figure out what happens to Søren once he confesses to his Jesuit superiors he's a daddy.

I'm sure he'll stay a priest. He will just be a priest in VERY BIG TROUBLE. I'd love to see him in exile and forced to do penance.

CYNDY: Is that happening for real?

TIFFANY: I don't know. It's alluded to in *The Queen* that Søren refuses to keep Fionn a dirty little secret so we know he's going to out himself.

CYNDY: I'd love to know what his penance in a [Pope] Francis era would be.

TIFFANY: But the consequences of said out-ting, I don't know. . . .

CYNDY: Oh, that I know, but I mean . . . are you definitely going to write that? And when? And will you screen share?

TIFFANY: Yeah, Pope Francis is cool. For those who aren't Catholic, Pope Francis made BIG news when he said that priestly celibacy was a discipline and not so much an order from God. More like fasting instead of like obeying the Commandments. It's good for you but not necessarily God-ordained of everyone [all priests, for example]. I would love to write that. But I don't know.

CYNDY: I'm thinking he could go teach at an all-girl school. Maybe that's what happened to that poor Jesuit who had to teach me for sophomore New Testament.

TIFFANY: Oh that poor priest. You as a student? I can't even.

CYNDY: I identified with Nora on many levels. Only I had zero interest in seducing him. Just annoying him.

TIFFANY: Happy to hear that. Nora and I have nothing in common except our senses of humor and hair color. Everyone thinks we're just the same. We couldn't be more different. I was a high school goody two shoes. Oh, and we're both Switches but Kingsley is also a Switch. Sadly no one ever mistakes me for King.

CYNDY: I picture her looking like you. I always get offended when people tweet you pictures of Rachel Weisz or whatever. But not acting like you.

TIFFANY: Rachel Weisz was MY choice to be Nora.

I wish I looked like Nora!

CYNDY: Again, we have to agree to disagree. ;)

TIFFANY: We can do that.

CYNDY: Although I'm coming around now to a white Kingsley. It only took eight books.

TIFFANY: I'll go on the record here to say I want Nikolaj Coster-Waldau to play Søren. I get asked that ALL the time.

CYNDY: I want an unknown.

TIFFANY: I promise if Kingsley were a black man I would not have talked about his huge cock so much. That's Stereotyping 101!

CYNDY: I have a very distinct idea of him in my head, and I never see anyone who fits it.

TIFFANY: That's okay. You picture who you want. As long as no one whitewashes Juliette or makes Nora tall.

CYNDY: Neither.

TIFFANY: We short girls have to stick together.

CYNDY: I literally picture you [as Nora].

TIFFANY: I wish! Actually not really.

CYNDY: Which is funny, since I didn't know what you looked like when I first read the books.

TIFFANY: If I were as sexy as Nora I'd never get any work done.

CYNDY: But I remember when I finally met you in person I was like, "Yup. EXACTLY Nora. Only slightly quieter."

TIFFANY: As she is a goddess, I'll take it as a compliment. As long as you call me Tiffany. Someone called me Nora and was offended when I asked to pretty please be called by my actual name. I do have to put my foot down when people start forgetting the books are fiction.

CYNDY: That would be weird.

TIFFANY: I know we don't want them to be . . . but they are.

CYNDY: I'm kind of glad they are. If they weren't, I think I'd become a celebrity stalker.

TIFFANY: I would certainly move to wherever Søren was pastoring, that's for sure.

CYNDY: I'd go to that Church. Not sure if I could bring myself to take Communion, but I'd at least go to Mass. And then think about it later. ;)

TIFFANY: I have this vision of the Original Sinners movies (there are no movies in the works by the way) and the very last scene of the very last movie would just be Nora lying on her back in bed after having been fucked and she just says to the camera, "God, I love being Catholic."

CYNDY: There would have to be a lot of fourth wall stuff.

TIFFANY: I think if there were more priests like Søren (meaning compassionate, not sexy) church attendance would skyrocket.

Oh yeah. I come so close to breaking the 4th wall in every book. Almost put "Reader, he fucked her" in *The King* but talked myself out of it.

CYNDY: Now I'm laughing imagining Søren turning to the camera and raising an eyebrow every time Nora or King was on screen . . . like in *The Office*.

TIFFANY: YES! Or *Parks and Rec*. He would be the Ben Wyatt of the Original Sinners, the one who thinks he's saner than everyone else but isn't.

CYNDY: But yes. We didn't even talk about "The Poinsettia." I can't be the only reader who contacts you saying, "Yeah, the Church bit is the most unrealistic part of these books." ;)

TIFFANY: I get a lot of, "I wish the Church was like this." But that's okay. There's a place for the aspirational in fiction.

CYNDY: One priest like Søren is a stretch, one who'd say Mass in a whorehouse?

TIFFANY: I feel like my characters have made me a better person. I've learned from them. Maybe someday I'll get an email from a baby priest who read my books and was inspired to be a little more open-minded.

Actually I know a famous Protestant pastor who gave a birthday party to a prostitute he met at a greasy spoon.

CYNDY: God, I hope so. Seems like the noobs (at least here) are reaching new levels of sanctimonious.

TIFFANY: So it can happen.

CYNDY: See again: Protestants.

TIFFANY: Good point. I have the convert's trouble in separating Catholic from Protestant as I've been both they are integrated in me.

CYNDY: I've often thought about trying out the Episcopalians—so close to Catholicism as to be familiar with none of the celibacy or LGBTQ+ weirdness. And women! Priests!

TIFFANY: Give it a shot! I'll go to church with you.

CYNDY: I make no secret of my giant crush on Amber Belldene [an Episcopalian priest who writes romance novels].

TIFFANY: God, I love Amber. Proof there is hope in this world for both romance AND the Church.

I loved writing Father Ballard in "The Confession of Marcus Stearns." It was fun to create Søren's second father.

CYNDY: There's a story. . . . I'd love a story that's just Søren confessing. Can you IMAGINE how long that would take?

TIFFANY: Søren's full confession? It would be longer than *The Mistress*.

TIFFANY: There are super hippie laid-back priests. There were more of them in the '60s and '70s in the post-Vatican II Jesus-freak era.

CYNDY: Oh, I've met some amazing priests. I don't hate them all.

TIFFANY: I know one who calls God "Father/Mother." "Our Father/Mother who art in Heaven . . ."

CYNDY: My father AND mother would pass right out in the pews.

TIFFANY: And he's OLD too. Not a young liberal priest. An OLD liberal priest.

CYNDY: Sometimes I think the old ones were the better ones.

TIFFANY: The young ones will be old ones someday. I'm hoping they mellow as they age. Don't we all?

CYNDY: I was a Cathedral kid . . . and one of the auxiliary bishops was the best. Living embodiment of "suffer the little children."

TIFFANY: Meaning I have mellowed with age. I'd still like to see Søren in a bishop's miter.

CYNDY: OMG. In the miter, Fionn on his shoulder.

TIFFANY: I could write that. The new bishop of Fairbanks, Alaska is a badass. Twenty years in the military as a chaplain. Hunts and fishes. Very handsome.

CYNDY: I haven't read anything about the new Bishop of Fairbanks. Obviously, I need to Google this.

TIFFANY: He gave the homily at the abbey I visited last weekend. Very cool guy.

CYNDY: OMG! Abbey! Was this your annual thing?

TIFFANY: Not annual but I would like it to be. I went to Mount Angel Abbey for a three-day silent retreat with the Benedictine monks there. There's a seminary there. BABYFACED priests. Oh my God, they're so young it hurts.

CYNDY: I'm thankful none of the retreats I ever went on or staffed was silent. I think I'd be dead.

TIFFANY: I can see that. The first night I was there, dinner wasn't silent. Silence began AFTER dinner. I sat at a random table with three random women, all retired and of course they all want to write a book now that they're retired. And I just sat there eating my pasta and thinking, "Please don't ask me what I do please don't ask me what I do . . ."

CYNDY: I was just going to ask if it was for writers or something. . . .

TIFFANY: Just Catholic women. Or any women. Non-Catholics can go on retreats as well as the abbey. They are very welcoming. But it cured me of my old ache to be a nun.

CYNDY: Not as much seduction as you'd thought?

TIFFANY: I could not handle those hours. I got up for Vigils at 4:45 on Saturday morning and thought I would die.

CYNDY: LOL.

TIFFANY: Father Pius said, "I came to the abbey 30 years ago because I wanted quiet, rest, peace and harmony. I got none of those but I'm still here."

So it opened my eyes a little.

My husband is pleased by this.

CYNDY: Father Pius?

TIFFANY: He ran our retreat. He's a monk/priest.

CYNDY: Given name?

TIFFANY: No. They pick their names when they take final vows, I believe.

CYNDY: Oh wait. You said Benedictine. I went to college with a guy who was entering the Basilians named Pius.

TIFFANY: A lot of them take their names from Popes and saints. But you never run across a Brother Sextus, do you? Or maybe YOU do. I don't.

CYNDY: LOL. No. At least they can choose them. My aunt (who left the convent) was assigned Bertilla. Who even knew there was a St. Bertilla?

TIFFANY: I'll have Søren do penance by joining a monastery. He can be Father Sextus. AWW YEAH. . . .

Søren is standing at my desk and shaking his head in a definite "No." He doesn't want to get up at 4:45 a.m. on a Saturday any more than I do.

CYNDY: The awesomeness of him getting assigned the name "Sextus." And Nora and King just CACKLING.

TIFFANY: I will find a way to work that into a story.

CYNDY: And having monogrammed stationery made [featuring the name "Sextus"] . . . And Griffin. OMG, the MILEAGE.

TIFFANY: Søren's like, "IT MEANS BORN SIXTH!"

CYNDY: -TY NINTH!

TIFFANY: Søren just sighed at me. It ruffled my hair.
He can sigh like a mother.
Did we hit all our topics?

CYNDY: Are you going to write that meeting in a Fionn book if it happens?

TIFFANY: Write the first meeting between Fionn and Søren?

CYNDY: And yes. That was the only question.

TIFFANY: Very tempting. I should at least write it from King's POV at some point. I don't know. But someday you will hear from Fionn.

CYNDY: So funny to think all those years ago I was not okay with *The Siren* [and rated it] four stars. You had too much in your pocket [that you didn't reveal until later books].

TIFFANY: Well, you had good reasons [for not giving it a full five stars]. I was playing the "long con." Writing is just one big long con game after all.

CYNDY: I'm still okay with four stars.

TIFFANY: Søren sends his regards, by the way. He says he'll get that fifth star out of you yet.

CYNDY: He can beat it out of me.

TIFFANY: I bet he would. But knowing him and you, he'd rather cut it out.

CYNDY: Dang.

TIFFANY: The only non-surgeon on earth with "obsidian blade scalpels" on his Christmas list. But that's Søren for you.

CYNDY: The sound I just made.

TIFFANY: I heard it.

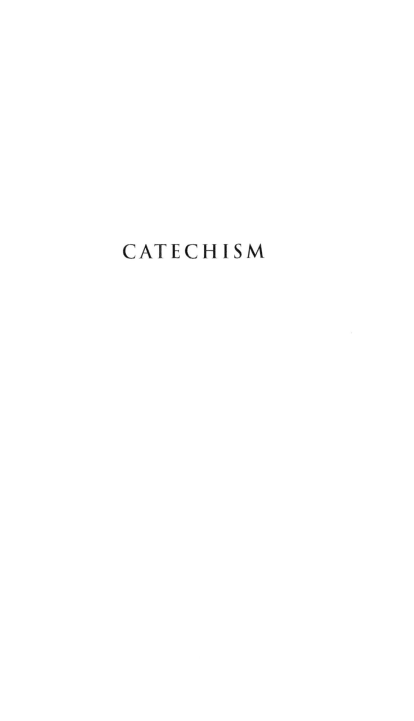

CATECHISM

21 FUN FACTS ABOUT FATHER MARCUS STEARNS AKA SØREN

1. All the names of the principle characters in *The Siren* are based on the four cardinal directions:

> Nora Sutherlin - North South
> Wes - West
> Zach Easton - East
> Søren - South

2. Søren's initials are kinky no matter which way you look at them:

> Søren Magnussen - SM (Sado-Masochism)
> Marcus Stearns - MS (Master-Slave)

3. Søren has two Ph.D.s—one in Theology and one in Canon Law. His full and correct title in the Catholic Church is rendered as "Reverend Doctor Marcus Stearns, S.J." The "S.J." stands for "Society of Jesus" which is the name of the religious order of priests Søren belongs to. They are commonly known as the Jesuits.

4. A man is considered a Jesuit from the moment he joins the order. Søren has been a Jesuit since age 18 upon entering the Society of Jesus. Not all Jesuits are priests, however. Søren was ordained into the priesthood at age 28. If he had not become a priest, he would still be a Jesuit brother.

5. Søren's name is either Søren Magnussen (his Danish name given to him by his mother) or Marcus Stearns (his legal name given to him by his father). He is never referred to as Søren Stearns or Marcus Magnussen.

6. Søren's middle name is Lennox, which is an authorial tribute to English soul singer Annie Lennox, who co-wrote the song "Missionary Man" from which the author of the Original Sinners series (Tiffany Reisz) took the phrase "Original Sinner." Lennox is also a district in Scotland.

7. Søren's son's name is derived from Fionn mac Cumhaill (rendered in English as Finn MacCool), an Irish mythological hero. The word "Fionn" means "blond." In *The King,* Søren tells Kingsley of an incident from his youth when a priest attempted to seduce him while they were translating the *Fiannaidheacht,* which is the cycle of Irish stories that includes the character Fionn mac Cumhaill. Grace Easton is half-Irish.

8. Søren is a polyglot, meaning he speaks and reads multiple languages. These include English, Danish, Swedish, French,

Spanish, Arabic, Hungarian, Italian, Japanese, German, Portuguese, Mandarin Chinese, and the biblical languages of Koine Greek, Hebrew, Aramaic, and Latin. Professor Henry Jones, i.e. Indiana Jones, inspired Søren's polyglotism.

9. Kingsley's "baptism" in *The King* is not a valid baptism as the words spoken by Søren are not the correct baptismal formula. The correct baptismal formula for a valid baptism in the Catholic Church must include the invocation of the Trinity, i.e. "I baptize you in the name of the Father, and the Son, and the Holy Spirit." Søren, being a good priest (most of the time) would not forcibly baptize anyone. He would, however, attempt to drown Kingsley for his own good.

10. Søren is a pescatarian—he eats no meat but does eat fish unless he's a guest in someone's home and then he eats what is served him.

11. Søren's motorcycle is a black 1992 Ducati 907 I.E. It is the only year the 907 I.E. came in black. As Jesuits take vows of poverty and live in community, they are not allowed to keep gifts unless given permission by their superiors. In *The King* Søren states he received permission to keep his motorcycle. Any of Søren's other "personal property" belongs to his Jesuit order or Sacred Heart, his parish in Connecticut.

12. The school where Søren trained for the priesthood is The Pontifical Gregorian University (or *Pontifica Università Gregorian* in Italian). It is located in Rome, Italy and was founded by the Jesuits. It is commonly referred to as the Gregorianum.

13. Søren's unique mix of sadism and compassion was based on God as He is portrayed in the Hebrew Bible (i.e. The Old Testament in the Christian Church). The first draft of *The Siren* was written while the author was attending a Methodist seminary.

14. Søren's father was a baron in the English aristocracy. As his father's only son, Søren could have claimed the title had he wished to leave the priesthood. He did not and the title is now in abeyance. The family estate is called Edenfell and is located in the north of England along the Scottish border. Due to Kingsley's largesse, Edenfell is now the property of Fionn Easton. Whether Fionn will attempt to claim the title and the estate remains to be seen. . . .

15. The scene in *The Mistress* where Søren walks to his possible death at dawn with Grace Easton was inspired by the walk with Aslan that Lucy and Susan undertake in *The Lion, The Witch, and The Wardrobe*, by C.S. Lewis. References to that work are scattered throughout the series.

16. The Sting song Søren and Eleanor waltz to in *The Saint* is "When We Dance." The Police song Nora dances to with Zachary at the end of *The Queen* is "Every Little Thing She Does is Magic."

17. Søren's correct birthdate is December 21, 1964, not December 21, 1965 as appears in *The Angel*. That was an uncorrected error. He is 51 years old during the present-day events of *The Queen*.

18. Søren's name is correctly pronounced "Suurn" (rhymes with Burn) in Danish. Nora, however, pronounces it the English way "Sore-ren" which is why in *The Saint* Søren says she pronounces his name "like an American." He answers to both English and Danish pronunciations.

19. Wakefield, Connecticut, home to Søren's parish Sacred Heart Catholic Church, is a fictional town. The name was taken from a small farming community in Kentucky near where the author lived at the time.

20. As revealed in *The King,* the 8 in the Eighth Circle logo is actually a letter S with a letter O around it and a slash through it. The S-O with slash is how Søren signs personal correspondence. Typographers refer to the ø in Søren's name as a "slashed o," and in Danish it is pronounced somewhat like the English "ur."

21. The original draft of *The Siren* was written in 2003. In the original draft, Nora picked Wesley over Søren. Søren told the author he didn't approve. The author changed the ending, because the author knows what's good for her.

ABOUT THE AUTHOR

Tiffany Reisz is the author of the internationally bestselling and award-winning Original Sinners series for Mira Books (Harlequin/Mills & Boon). Tiffany's books inhabit a sexy shadowy world where romance, erotica, and literature meet and do immoral and possibly illegal things to each other. She describes her genre as "literary friction," a term she stole from her main character, who gets in trouble almost as often as the author herself.

She lives in Louisville, Kentucky. If she couldn't write, she would die.

Like Tiffany Reisz on Facebook: www.facebook.com/littleredridingcrop

Follow 8th Circle Press on Twitter: @8thcirclepress

Visit www.tiffanyreisz.com for free short stories, and to subscribe to the Tiffany Reisz e-mail newsletter

Printed in Great Britain
by Amazon

43263199R00081